About the author

After a roving early life Mollie de Goris worked in the Bodleian Library, Oxford, for twenty years. She is married and lives on the Costa del Azahar in Spain.

FORTHCOMING

Reputation, a novel in two parts
By Mollie de Goris

THE DON'S WIFE'S TALE

A novel

By
Mollie de Goris

Followed by four tales of fact and fiction

Pharos Oxford

First published in 1999 by the Pharos Press

Pharos Press
220 Woodstock Road,
Oxford OX2 6QA

ISBN 0 9535453 0 X

Designed and produced in Great Britain by
Axxent Ltd,
The Short Run Book Company,
St Stephen's House,
Arthur Road,
Windsor,
Berkshire SL4 1RY

CONTENTS

For 'Janice'

THE DON'S WIFE'S TALE

'My dear Emmie, how can you be so gullible – to believe for a moment that they'd refund your fees...'

'But advertised in the *Radio Times*, Walter. And of course I wouldn't want my money back – the refund is simply guaranteed if one hasn't earned as much by the end of the course. Just listen again, dear...'

'Guaranteed indeed. Wait till you read the small print. What does the Don's wife say?'

'Oh for goodness sake, Walter, why can't you call her Janice? And I don't doubt she'll be as discouraging as you are.'

'Well dear, my advice is to forget it, – and now would you mind passing the marmalade?'

'Orange or grapefruit?'

'The tall jar, – it's only to prop up *The Times.* So let's see...One across: – "Aquarius is gregarious"...five letters...'

'Oxford 98245'

'Janice it's me...'

'Emmie, how nice...'

'Isn't it funny, Jan, how we always know who we are...each other, I mean...'

'My dear, after all these years! So what goes on in the country?'

'I need to talk to you, Jan, while Walter is outside.'

'Does Walter enjoy being at home?'

'He's O.K. for the moment, sawing logs. But what I want to tell you, Jan, is that I'm sending away for that Course.'

'Course? Which course?'

'The Writing Course, I told you about the advert...'

'My dear Emmie, I've already told you – I've no faith in a correspondence school teaching one how to write.'

'Janice! Stop being so academic and pompous! I'm sure I can learn a lot. Anyway I get two weeks free trial, – and there's the money-back guarantee – if I don't earn my fees by the end of the course...'

'Well dear, be careful how you commit yourself, – and don't be too trusting about the guarantee...'

'It seems to me it's the school that's trusting. They actually trust you to tell them what you get published. One could keep it dark and demand the fees back anyway.'

'That could never happen, Em. All writers are proud of getting into print. No new writer could resist telling.'

'Trust you to say something wise!'

'Experience of university life, dear. And the higher the academic level the greater the conceit, – you'd never believe...'

'Yes, yes, – so you've often told me. But the thing is, Jan, – besides the bliss of earning money, I need something to do of my very own...'

'I'm not surprised. Your isolated life would kill me'

'Well, of course, while Walter was working the house and garden were my own thing. But since he retired he is into everything – inside and out, and always needing my help. You know how men are, – can't manage the most simple job single-handed. I can hardly call my soul my own, let alone the garden or the house. But I daren't discourage him, – he's making such a brave effort to adjust.'

'Adjust, Emmie? You said Walter was longing to retire...'

'Ah, but it's different when it happens, Jan, – so suddenly and so much earlier than expected. I'm not grumbling, you know, he is perfectly sweet, really. Have you let Sue's flat?'

'Hopefully. The agent has found a couple of academic women who might suit. I'm going to show them over this afternoon...'

'But Jan, academics will turn the place into a slum! Sorry dear... I know you don't. How is Sue?'

'Fine, though she's none too keen on Huston. Well, Em, I must fly, on account of those academic hags. I only wish Alec would take a turn with the chores. You don't know when you are lucky...'

'Do ring me soon, Jan. I'd like to hear how your women turn out.'

'Walter, I have decided to go ahead with it.'

'Have you indeed! Then I hope you've read the small print carefully.'

'Can't find any. The guarantee is written all over, – in block capitals.'

'Well my dear, if you're determined to squander your money I can't stop you. Only don't expect me to subsidise your whims when your nest egg is used up.'

'But Walter, I might be able to make some money, and even at worst I shall get my money back.'

'Good God, woman, you are naïve. Pass the marmalade!'

'Binns End 201'

'Emmie!'

'Jan! I've been wondering about you. How did you get on with your academic hags last week?'

'They weren't hags after all, Emmie, quite the reverse, academic certainly, both are doing research and one is writing a book. But you should have seen them, Em. Such a surprise...sophisticated, exquisitely turned out...'

'Really, they are young then?'

'Well, not in the first flush, the mid-thirties I should say. But their clothes, Em! As a matter of fact they gave Harrods bank as a reference, and you can just see...makes me long to dash up to London and change my whole wardrobe.'

'Don't I know the feeling! They like Sue's flat, of course?'

'Yes, they are delighted because in agents' terms it's a maisonette, you know, with its own front door. The only problem was fitting their Merc into Sue's garage...'

'Murk?'

'A Mercedes, dear, – the sleek open one. Anyway is does fit. And Em, another happy coincidence, – they need the flat for exactly the time Sue is away, so no more bother about that. And such a stimulating contact! I must ask them for drinks as soon as they are settled in.'

'You are lucky, Jan, living in Oxford. But I've had an engrossing week too, filling in my self-analysis form...'

'Self-analysis? Whatever for?'

'For my correspondence course. I have decided to go ahead, Jan, so don't try to put me off. The first thing you have to do is fill up this form, four pages, no less. Questions all about yourself so they can match you with the most suitable tutor...'

'Good heavens, Emmie, it sounds like a dating service!'

'Yes, exciting isn't it? I can't wait to be paired up.'

'Whatever does Walter make of it all?'

'Well he affects not to notice, he is so cross I can't talk to him. But now that I've actually paid he won't want me to waste the money, – so it gives me a licence to write, as it were. Walter has become so careful since he retired.'

'Walter careful? I can't believe it!'

'You know he was always excessive, Jan. Expansive when he had money, and obsessively careful now of course, when he thinks he hasn't, and I'm certainly not complaining, it would have been much worse the other way round. Anyway he was visibly impressed when my trial package arrived. Seven text-books and a super file packed with practical advice. And for someone like me, stuck away in the country, it's all very stimulating, – so don't dare to be snooty...'

'Emmie dear, I don't want to discourage you, but won't you soon get bored? Will you really be able to struggle through to the end? Oh Lord, there I go again...'

'Your life is so varied, Jan. You might be buried in the eighteenth century with your work but you do see life all round you. I'm just buried in the country.'

'But why didn't you simply try writing? I intend to when I can find the time. I want to try my hand at a thriller. Suspense, Emmie, that's my thing, and I keep thinking up plots...'

'Jan, it's not fair! You are so gifted, – and I haven't been able to think up one plot yet. Luckily they only ask me to analyse a popular magazine for my first assignment...'

'Assignment, Emmie?'

'Janice, you mustn't laugh! you are the only person I can talk to...'

'So, – four across: "Young sucker temporarily unnattracted by hunting." In eight letters...Hmm...'

'You know, Walter, this magazine quite defies analysis, – and they ask one to figure out how it is put together...'

'Aha! "Offshoot." So where are we with ten down?'

'Well let's hope they can teach me how to write, – they are certainly making me think...I shall have to organise my thoughts, though. Good heavens – I might end up with a concentrated mind!'

'Something amusing you, Emmie?'

'Yes indeed... Weren't you listening?'

'H'mm... "Wild horseman decapitated in Liguria." Decapitated...? What were you saying, dear? Liguria...?

'Oh nothing, Walter, – forget it.'

Oxford 98245'

'Janice, you haven't rung for ages, and it was your turn.'

'My dear Emmie, I've been so pressed.'

'Well I've got something to tell you, – and I've been longing to hear more about your glamorous women. What does Alec make of them?'

'He hasn't had the chance to make anything so far, – they are so involved with research just now they won't accept invitations. In fact I've just this moment come in after an abortive attempt to call on them. Sue wanted me to collect some papers, but I couldn't get any answer – though I felt sure there was someone inside the flat. And a most disturbing thing, Emmie. There was a young man in a red sports car parked outside the gate, and you know what? He has followed me home...'

'So you haven't lost your touch, Jan!'

'Oh don't be silly, Emmie, – though it could hardly be by chance over such an intricate route, – and he is still parked outside. I can see him through the window.'

'You think he is casing your joint?'

'I don't know what to think. He's certainly not trying to hide himself, – not furtive. I'd better alert the porter though.'

'Alert poor old Cedric? Is that possible?'

'Ah, the car is driving away, perhaps it was coincidence after all.'

'Nothing so exciting here. All that moves outside my window is a chaffinch...and three blackbirds disputing territory...'

'You'll be able to write nature stories, Em.'

'I don't know if I could bear to, – it is such a deadly game, when you come to think. Only one blackbird can live in one territory, – the other two might not even survive the winter. No comfortable retirement for birds.'

'You said you have things to tell?'

'Well just the one thing, that's why I rang. Jan, I've been introduced to my tutor!'

'Not in the flesh?'

'No, of course not. But Jan, it's just like having a new friend...better in a way, not being able to see him...I can let my imagination roam. I can even imagine myself differently...'

'How nice for you! I feel quite jealous. How is the actual writing?'

'Well that is the crunch, of course. They advise you to write what you are doing, – so I am just writing down as I go along, – which has a weird effect, like one looking-glass opposite another, – giving endless reflections...'

'Just as well Walter doesn't take any interest! Isn't he feeling neglected?'

'Well luckily he enjoys mending things, and often he gets so engrossed he forgets to ask me for help...except when he's cooking...'

'Walter cooking? I can't believe it!'

'The television has made him interested, – worse luck, – since I am kitchen-maid.'

'I don't know about worse luck, Em. If only Alec would do the cooking once in a while I'd gladly settle for the washing-up!'

'I hate to disturb the magnum opus, Emmie, but you can't expect me to do everything at once you know! This recipe needs scalded milk. Could you come and watch that it doesn't boil...'

'Just a moment, Walter...'

'Emmie!'

'All right! I'm *coming*!'

'And now you're here, dear, would you just put a hand on my bowl, – it keeps spinning round when I beat...only for God's sake! – you are taking your eye off the milk!'

'Binns End 201'

'Emmie! My dear, I've just had another disturbing experience...'

'Good heavens Jan! The man in the red car again?'

'No, – though it is connected with those women. You know I'd called twice to collect Sue's papers without getting any answer? Well today I went again, and this time the garage door was open and the Merc gone. I rang the bell several times, – but the place felt empty, – so I decided to use my door-key and go in. After all I am the owner's mother...'

'What did you find inside?'

'All beautifully kept, Em. No need to poke about on that score. But I unlocked the cupboard under Sue's desk feeling just like a burglar, – and then when I found what I was looking for, the telephone rang, right next to me, – gave me an awful guilty start – and like an idiot I picked up the receiver automatically. I didn't intend to keep my visit secret of course. It might have been helpful to answer...'

'I should have just been plain curious. Who was it?'

'A man, Emmie, who asked if I was Betty. I said I wasn't, but that I would take a message, and asked his name. At that he gave what I can only describe as a dirty laugh, and said that perhaps in the circumstances he had better just call himself Fred! And then, Emmie, – I can't tell you exactly what came next, – I thought he was trying to make an appointment...until I realised that it was one of those obscene phone calls we keep hearing about!'

'Oh Jan, how horrible! What did you do?'

'Why I slammed down the receiver, and locked Sue's desk, and got myself out of the flat as fast as I could.'

'You didn't take down his message, then?'

'Emmie, don't laugh. We read about these things but you can't imagine how unnerving it is when they actually happen...I still feel quite shaken...it never happened to me before...'

'Well it wouldn't, I suppose, with Alec's name in the book. What does Alec think?'

'I won't tell him. No purpose in getting him or anyone else worked up when nothing can be done. You are the only person I can talk to, Em. I must try to think of other things. How goes the writing? How did you manage your article?'

'My dear, all I could think of was the time the washing-machine caught fire –which is no joke when you live where I do, – half a mile from the nearest house, even if I were crow...'

'Yes, yes, I remember you telling me about it. So what is your next assignment?'

'A short story, Jan. The most profitable outlet, they say, only I can't think of a single plot. They tell you how to construct plots, but not what plots to construct. Walter thinks I'm slacking...'

You don't seem to be making much progress with your scribbling, Emmie.'

'I'm trying to think up a plot, Walter. Have you got any ideas?'

'Of course not, my dear, – I accept my limitations. The only grand illusions I suffer from are yours. I knew from the beginning how this one would end.'

'Quiet, Walter. Don't nag, – I've told you, I am thinking.'

'Binns End 201'

'Emmie!'

'But Jan! Wasn't it my turn?'

'I've got the most incredible news for you, Emmie, – if I can manage to be coherent... Those women, – they've decamped! And you simply won't believe this, – they were not academic at all, – it seems they've been running the place as a Massage Parlour...!'

'Never! You surely don't mean...?'

'Indeed I do!'

'Jan! How absolutely killing!'

'Oh hilarious, you'll fall about when you hear. It's made me quite hysterical, – I don't know where to begin...'

'Begin at the beginning, Jan. How did you hear?'

'Well to begin with from the agent. It seems they hadn't paid the rent last month, – he thought they might have gone away on holiday and that I might know for how long. Well I didn't, of course, but I do know how absent-minded researchers can be, so I tried to reassure him. He was uneasy because it is not just the rent, you know, he has to pay all the condominium charges, plus the central heating, which comes to a fearful whack, I can tell you. That's why Sue needs to keep the place let...'

'Yes, yes, you've told me. What happened then?'

'Well the cleaning woman goes in twice a week for the morning, and it seems she'd been given a key, because they didn't get up early...'

'Not surprising!'

'...and this morning when she found they'd gone she rang the agent, and he rang me, and I told him I'd go to have a look as soon as I could get away, about five o'clock...'

'And none of you had any idea then?'

'Not the slightest, Emmie, I'm telling you. Well when I got there I went straight upstairs, and found it was quite true. The beds were not made and the wardrobes were empty with their doors hanging open. It was dark by then and the windows had gone huge and black, quite spooky, like in a film, and when the telephone by the bed rang suddenly again, right next to me, it sent a shock-wave through me that nearly riveted me to the floor...'

'Jan! I can just feel it!'

'It's true, I went quite stiff for a moment, though by the time I picked up the receiver, my hand was shaking. It was a man again...'

'The same voice?'

'No, quite different, upper class. But I was afraid to talk to him, Emmie. I was so unnerved after the last call and all the odd coincidences I felt I must collect my wits before speaking to anyone, – so I just said the first thing that came into my head. I told him I was engaged for the moment, and asked him to ring back in about fifteen minutes. At which he gave a kind of chortle and replied, 'Oh I think we'd better give you longer than that!'

'Jan how priceless!'

'Well it didn't mean a thing to me at the time, – and then the doorbell rang...'

'An early evening client?'

'No, thank God. It was the cleaning woman back again. She'd had no money either, – for four weeks. I took her inside and paid her of course. She told me she suspected that there was nobody upstairs this morning because the phone kept ringing and it wasn't answered from the bedroom as usual. They had told her not to do upstairs and never to answer the phone. But at last she went up to have a look...'

'Had she suspected anything else?'

'My dear no, a nice young woman. We were a couple of innocents together, only enraged about losing our money. Anyway she couldn't stop because of her children, – and as I was letting her out who should be there again but the young man in the red sports car! He asked if he could have a word with me. He seemed quite respectable so I invited him in, – I thought he was another creditor…A pleasant young man…'

'Don't tell me he was a customer!'

'No, nor was he a burglar. He turned out to be a reporter, though to begin with I didn't guess that either…'

'A reporter? How interesting, – for which paper?'

'Free lance, just beginning to make his way, but such a thing didn't occur to me so I had no idea what his questions were leading up to…such subtle questions! I predict that young man will go far, Em. He was building up the story, you see, and was curious to find out how I was connected…'

'Jan! You don't mean he took you for Madame?'

'I really believe he did. He had found out where I live and who I am, and I don't flatter myself he could have taken me for the other thing. But Emmie, can you imagine the scandal? Can you imagine the headlines? "Don's Wife runs 'Massage Parlour" And just when Alec is well in the running for Master! Imagine how Horace would crow! They are neck and neck at the moment…'

'What happened? How did you find out who he was? The reporter?'

'Well there was another telephone call, – a different voice again. Would you believe, Emmie that there are so many sex-starved males about, – ready to pay, – in these days! I wonder what they charged?'

'You didn't find out? But do get on Jan, I am dying to hear…'

'My dear, I didn't learn any practical details. In fact it must have been so obvious that I was talking at cross-purposes that the reporter suddenly came across the room and took the receiver out of my hand and said to the caller, 'You've got the wrong number, chum.' And he left the receiver off the hook!'

'Lucky you'd asked him in! What then?'

'Well he asked if he could make me a cup of tea while he told me all about it. There was something so comforting in the mention of tea, Em, I felt reassured at once. Though as it happened we found they'd left a bottle of gin behind, and we weighed into that instead.'

'What did he tell you?'

'He began at his beginning, of noticing an advertisement in a London paper and recognising the Oxford code. He suspected that the so-called massage was a front and found out from a telephone call that indeed it was...'

Did he make an appointment?'

'Well he didn't admit, – certainly not, judging by the high moral tone he took in the article he wrote, which he showed me...'

'In the London paper?'

'No, he hasn't got that far yet, – it was printed in one of those free newspapers which are pushed through letter-boxes in Oxford. Cedric gets ours of course so I never see them.'

'But perhaps your women did?'

'Yes he supposed that might have frightened them off, – but more probably that they had reached the limit of easy credit and were being dunned. Poor Sue! The young man is hoping to trace them to continue his story, but he doesn't think we'll ever get any money.'

'Oh Jan, how I'd have loved to be in on your cosy chat!'

'Cosy! I was so knocked up I felt quite ginny in the end, Em. I really shouldn't have driven home, but one does of course, and I did. That could have caused a fine old scandal too. "Don's Wife on Drunk Driving Charge"! But I was dying to tell Alec, and expecting him to be home and hungry, – no hope of him doing the cooking. But he hasn't come in yet, and I couldn't keep the news to myself. Besides, you know so much already which Alec does not...'

'So the obscene phone-call...?'

'A genuine enquirer, without doubt!'

'Have you left the telephone off the hook?'

'Yes. But you know, Em, by the time I'd drunk a couple of gins I felt a great curiosity to listen in. No chance of that though, – the moral young man would not have approved. He saw me out and helped me lock the garage and everything, and told me to get the telephone number changed...'

'You could have a little listen before they do.'

'It makes me shudder really, Emmie, – but you know what, the story is already developing in my mind as fiction. Just think, Em if I had recognised one of those voices...someone I know well...'

'You mean like Walter?'

'Well, no... I can't quite imagine Walter, nor yet Alec. But Horace! I wouldn't put anything past him, even when he is running for Master. And I could have led him on, you know, in order to blackmail him! Prevent him from being a candidate. Can't you see the story shaping, Emmie? This time I really must get the idea written up and sent off. I could change the background to Cambridge...'

'Jan! It is really not fair! You've got a plot and I can't think of any!'

'Never mind, Em, I'm sure a good idea will turn up...Oh there is Alec now, I must fly. But don't feel too anxious about the writing, Emmie. You can always get your fees back if you don't succeed.'

'Janice!'

EMMIE IN ABANO

'Binns End 201'

'Emmie dear, we're off, – that is first thing in the morning...'

'Oh Jan, I do so envy you...'

'Well, as you know, I'm none too keen on a jaunt round the States, – but a lecture tour is a God-send for Alec just now, – to get him over his rage and disappointment. He simply can't stand the sight of Horace pontificating at High Table, – in fact he's hardly dined in Hall since, – so I shall be more than glad of a break from cooking...'

'And you'll see Sue!'

'Yes, of course. Only for a few days though, we are going to meet at Palm Springs...'

'Oh Jan, how blissful that sounds in this freezing weather, – you know Walter couldn't get to his aunt's funeral because of the snow.'

'I wondered, I was going to ask. Was he an executor?'

'No, she died intestate, poor old thing, so they couldn't even cremate her. In fact the first we heard of her death was the undertaker ringing up to ask what to do with the body...'

'There might be a little windfall for Walter, perhaps?'

'Alas no, she lived on a small annuity. Walter thinks he will be responsible for her debts.'

'Oh surely not, Emmie.'

'Well you know Walter, – the soul of honour if anything is owing. No Palm Springs for us I'm afraid. Are they hot springs, – like Abano Terme in Italy? I've just been reading about them. Hot water gushing out of a mountain, just right for swimming in...'

'But Walter, there is the house at least – which should pay for the funeral and the bills, with something left over perhaps...'

'Probably mortgaged to the hilt, Emmie. Nobody could have lived so many years on such a devalued annuity. My guess is that she was advised to realise some capital by mortgaging the house, and she lived on that in the end...'

'Poor Aunt Jessie. It must be awful to have money worries when you are old.'

'You can say that again!'

'Why can't we live on capital from our house, Walter?'

'Oh don't talk about things you don't understand, Emmie. We are too young.'

'Well that's a comfort!'

'Oxford 98245'

'Jan, you are back! And you haven't rung! I've been longing to talk ...'

'My dear Emmie, – we only got in last night, after a frustrating trip...I'm not sure it's done Alec any good at all.'

'So you hinted on your cards. But it's us I want to talk about...Walter and me...'

'Good God, Emmie, you haven't decided to leave him at last?'

'Oh don't be absurd, Jan, of course I wouldn't do that. Especially now. Walter's taken on a new lease of life...'

'Congratulations! But if it's from anything like an injection of hormones don't let Alec hear of it. I'm glad to be over that sort of thing.'

'Jan! Stop leaping to conclusions and let me get a word in. You remember Walter's Aunt Jessie died just before you left?'

'The one who left him all her debts?'

'Yes, only she didn't, in spite of her small annuity, which died with her of course. And even better the house turned out to be unencumbered...a dismal barn of a place, if you ask me. But you know what? It fetched well over two hundred thousand, – for development!'

'Emmie dear! That is what I call a new lease of life!'

'Well you know, Walter had become so adjusted to economising I was afraid it might be too late for him to adjust back. He was already worrying about death duties and capital gains tax. But he made a discovery in Aunt Jessie's garage. You will never guess what!'

'A Roller? Or a Merc?'

'Nothing so ordinary, dear. He found Uncle Albert's cherished Delage, built in the early thirties...'

'Not still working, surely?'

'Indeed yes, it seems the car has been carefully maintained by a specialist garage. They told us Aunt Jessie wouldn't hear of selling, – for sentimental reasons. That's what I meant by a new lease of life. It has simply given Walter his youth back!'

'I remember when we were young he had a taste for exotic cars. But he'll get engrossed with it, Emmie. You will just end up a veteran-car widow, – I've seen it all before. They never stop cleaning them and can't bear to go out on the road...'

'Well you are wrong for a change. Walter has planned a Continental tour. The Hovercraft tickets are all booked and paid for.'

'Now you are making me envious. What route will you take?'

'Not quite decided yet. I can't risk an outright suggestion because Walter is so counter-suggestible. But I am working on it. I want to swim in some thermal springs...'

'You left one of your glossies among my car magazines, Emmie.'

'So that's where it went!'

'I see it's a special number on European spas. They describe them as the last outposts of elegance and a more leisured age. The era of the Delage, when you come to think, Emmie. Perhaps we should take in a few before they get spoiled too...'

'That sounds expensive dear.'

'We can afford to spread ourselves now, you know darling, – and you really deserve a bit of pampering.'

'Poor Aunt Jessie!'

'You know Emmie, I do believe we have her blessing. She must have had something in mind, leaving a legacy like that, keeping the car a secret all this time in such perfect order.'

'Binns End 201'

'Just to wish you bon voyage, Em. So you won the first round over the watering holes?'

'It was Walter's own suggestion. It seems they are the only places left in the world which fit the image of the Delage and himself driving it.'

'Cunning creature!'

'Well you should know how marriage is. We gain a few and lose a few.'

'You'll find plenty of copy for your writing.'

'The funny thing is, Jan, – now that life is actually happening to me I don't feel the urge to write any more.'

'But your tutor? The one you were having a romantic flutter with? Won't you be letting him down?'

'He turned out to be a woman, Jan. She is called Leslie, you see, and I never thought…I did feel such a fool…'

'You will write to me, I hope.'

'From every stop, I promise.'

At Schlagenbad

Dear Janice,

We have arrived at our first watering-hole as you call them. It took several days to get here but the car has behaved perfectly. This is a little spa in the hills near Wiesbaden, – which Walter refers to as 'Shag-in-bed' having become quite skittish, as if on honeymoon, – only he would never have used a term like that in those days, and now of course his honeymoon and love-affair is with his machine. I merely bask in the fringe glow which is very pleasant and relaxing.

But it's amazing how travelling in a period vehicle alters one's life style. We can hardly pause in traffic without collecting a crowd and even for the briefest stop she can never be left unguarded. 'She' is a super sports job with a long bonnet held down by a hefty leather strap across the middle. It is tough luck on me that Uncle Albert didn't opt for one of the elegant Delage saloons in which I could have worn glamorous clothes, though the rig we do wear is very flattering. A kind of soft leather flying-suit of the period with fur-trimmed helmet and goggles, in which Walter looks positively handsome, and I do believe knocks a few years off my image, especially with the goggles down.

You may be sure that wherever we arrive stabling is top priority. Never mind if the wife is comfortable as long as the motor is safely bedded down. And no question of booking in advance. Our touring must conform to the days when motorists just drove nonchalantly into a place and looked over the hotels. Luckily it is so early in the season.

On our second night Walter had no luck getting garage-space, probably because he enquired for that first while I was left guarding the car. So we drove on and on, – you know how it goes, and at last we reached an old coaching inn and I was so tired and cross I leapt out of the car first and Walter had to stay. I entered the foyer ripping off my flying-helmet and flinging my gloves on the desk, as 1930-ish as you please, demanding a double-room with bath and sitting-room en suite, on the quiet side of the house.'

'Certainly, Madame,' replied the clerk.

'And we need secure accommodation for a valuable car.'

At this there was a hurried conference inside the office. Strange how in half-empty hotels the garage space is always full up, and it was the manager himself who moved out his car. But as soon as the staff saw the Delage they were ready to do all they could for our comfort. I have taken note for the future.

Here in Schlagenbad we have found a modest hostelry with a spacious garage. We arrived yesterday and learned from people who strolled up to admire the car that the early evening custom is to visit the indoor pool which can be seen projecting from the trees lower down the valley.

So with the car safely tucked up we walked down through the woods to find the entrance and going in from a chilly spring evening were enveloped in a hot-house atmosphere with an ambience which made Walter jolly with the receptionist. She told him that men had to wear bathing-caps too. He bought himself one. 'Do I need a small one for my moustache?' he asked. 'The moustache it is not necessary to cover,' the girl replied seriously.

'I suppose moustaches get disinfected with all that beer,' said Walter, putting on his cap when we met again beside the pool. 'But good heavens Emmie, look at that chap!'

A bald-headed man with a bushy black beard and a huge stomach slung out over brief bathing-trunks, was covering his shining bald head with a cap, carefully tucking in a few wisps of hair still growing round his neck. Then he lowered himself, beard and all, gently into the pool. There is a large notice saying that diving and splashing are verboten.

The pool is a bizarre glass-fronted rounded structure projecting from the wooded hill so that walking round the wide promenade on the window side is rather scary with no apparent support underneath and the valley sloping steeply below. Looking down inwards the huge pool appears like an amphibious ballroom in which nobody swims, couples gyrate sedately, giving a dream-like impression. Walter and I lowered ourselves into the warm soothing water, and we also gyrated gently, smiling at each other, hardly daring to laugh. Oddly enough when we emerged we felt hungry as if we had been swimming into the Atlantic.

We dined in a restaurant with a German band and a small dance-floor, nothing like as big as the pool. The public all seemed to be German, all as stolid as the food. We are what we eat I thought as I ate. But one woman was dressed elegantly and she was outstanding. 'Look at that couple,' I said, 'I wonder what nationality?'

Walter half-turned his head. 'That nondescript man? They are English, staying in our hotel, – he drives a Rover.' This summed them up as far as my husband was concerned.

I pointed out that the woman was beautiful and was certainly wearing model clothes, but Walter wasn't prepared to twist his neck for a glimpse of haute-couture, and cannot interest himself in femmes fatales in his present state of mind.

Then while we were having coffee a middle-aged German came to our table an asked me to dance. Well I was so astonished I accepted. The band struck up a rousing tune and we went careering round the little floor, spinning in circles so fast I kept taking off. My partner seemed to enjoy it hugely but I was extremely giddy by the time I sat down again. The man beamed and indicated that he must quench his thirst, but Walter looked too forbidding and I was too flustered to do anything about it. The man snapped his heels again and departed. 'Why did he chose me?' I wondered.

'No doubt he is paid for it, – and picked you out as the lightest weight,' my gallant spouse replied. And looking about and sizing up the other women I was forced to agree in my mind, – the English couple had left earlier. 'But I must say, Emmie,' said Walter, taking another, obviously a new look at me, 'You are looking very well just now, – the holiday must be doing you good.'

Indeed it is!

Today was much warmer and I went alone to the open swimming-pool which is reached through the hotel garden. But out of doors the naturally warm water felt hardly luke and made me shiver as I lowered myself gingerly down the steps. There swimming is allowed and after striking out vigorously I began to enjoy it, but couldn't keep up long, – not in training yet. The deck-chairs were all occupied and wet bodies were strewn around the pool edge lying on towels, so having made my towel wet trying to dry myself I did the same.

A nice Frau spread out her towel next to me and supposed that I was English. 'How did you guess?' I asked. 'From your figure of course, I am filled with envy.' Well, having my figure envied is an experience forgotten these many years, and here was a second compliment in as many days. Everything is relative I suppose and lying next to this ample woman I did feel quite slim. She turned out to be Dutch and told me that she came here regularly for chronic rheumatic pains, – which didn't surprise me. I'm sure I'd get chronic pains too if I lay about in a wet bathing-costume on a wet towel. The sun was quite warm but the cold penetrated from underneath.

So to avoid becoming chronically crippled too and waste my entrance fee I opted for another swim, and this time the water felt quite warm, but I could see my goose-pimples generating little bubbles all over me, so I swam about briskly to scatter them. Suddenly there came a deafening crack of lightning and the water was pitted with heavy raindrops. A black cloud had loomed in over the mountain with a thunderstorm which emptied the deck-chairs and sent people scurrying for cover or diving into the pool like seals. The water was afoam with splashing bodies. But the lightning, Jan, and the noise! I expected we'd all be electrocuted any minute, the way they kill fish. I got myself out and fled back here, and now of course as soon as I am safely dry the sun is shining strongly again. I have just ordered tea. Ah, here it is, and Walter too.

'That couple with the Rover have just left...'

'Here is some tea, dear. Good heavens, – they expect me to brew it, with a pot of hot water and tea-bags in a saucer!'

'...they are called Elliot. The wife came over to look at the Delage...'

'That gorgeous creature with the lovely clothes!'

'Well I can't say I noticed what she was wearing. But an extraordinary thing, Emmie. She said that her grandfather had a Delage, a saloon, which she'd give anything to drive about in now, – for sentimental reasons...'

'I wouldn't object to a saloon either, – for practical reasons.'

'And you know what? Their next stop is Baden-Baden too, – there's a coincidence! What were you saying dear?'

'Did she say where they intend to stay in the twin Badens?'

'A hotel on a street somewhere, – very plush it sounds, but not much good for garaging, she thinks, so we will have to search further. She says she will look out for the Delage and just said Au revoir.'

At Baden-Baden

Dear Janice,

No wonder they call it Baden-Baden! Baden once could hardly do justice to so much opulence, though in fact it is simply because there were two Baden families. But my dear the prices! The full cure turns out to be prohibitive, even if we needed it, but we are letting Aunt Jessie treat us to a drink of the water. We haven't seen anything yet of the woman who admired the Delage, no doubt she is involved with some beauty treatment.

In the meanwhile Walter and I are enjoying the peripheral delights. We stroll in the morning to the Kurhaus and Casino which are housed in one building, white-columns outside and positively dazzling within. Cool glittering fountains, various lush gaming-rooms, and the 'Hall of a thousand candles', Louis XIII, all beige and gold, – and in the grand old frescoed Trinkhalle we take our trink of the famous water. Grape-juice is also offered which no doubt tastes nicer, but we can't waste the chance of drinking the water from"its source.

The afternoon is Walter's time for tending the Delage and then I wander round the ruins of the Roman baths or around the palace of the Margraves looking at the silver, crystal and Meissen.

Just now I am sitting in the Café-Konditorei-Konig which is something of an institution like Florians's of Venice. I am intent on indulging myself with some of their famous pastries, – and I can tell you, after so much walking this is the best moment of the day. Ah here come the cakes now. I shall soon be fat as a frau.

'Are you enjoying yourself here Emmie'

'Very much, though I prefer swimming in water to drinking it.'

'Mrs Elliot and her husband came to look at the Delage again. Wasn't it clever of her to find it? She tells me they are inclined to move on. They are booked at a spa called Abano in Italy on the sixteenth, but think of going to a place called Saint Something-or-other on Lake Garda, for a couple of days first. She says it is a charming spot and was suggesting we drove there with them, but Elliot said he doubted if he could keep up with my beast. I must say I feel tempted to show him a bit of pace. So where are the maps, dear? What do you say?'

At St Sirmione

My dear Janice,

Here we are in a little hotel on the island of St Sirmione on Lake Garda which we had never heard of before. It was suggested to Walter by a couple called Elliot who had interested themselves in the Delage The island is attached to the mainland by a bridge which I look down on from our balcony. And this bridge is the king-pin of to-day's letter.

We arrived two days ago but Mr Elliot avoided travelling with us, making an excuse which I thought genuine, of having to wait for a telephone call. 'Dismal timid chap,' said Walter, 'he is obviously afraid of competing with the Delage in his Rover.'

We came over the Brenner Pass and I too was happy not to be in a race. But as we neared the end of the autostrada leading to Garda the Elliot's Rover pulled gently past us, he driving and she waving. As you might guess Walter immediately gave chase, but for all his clamping his foot to the floorboard the Rover gradually diminished in the distance! This was terrible, unforgivable! We left the autostrada but Walter still drove on fiercely, concentrating on hating poor Mr Elliot, while I hung on tightly trying to concentrate on the signposts, until we came at last to the little bridge which connects the island of St Sirmione to a peninsular.

Walter drove up to the bridge gate which was shut. On the land side was a large car-park with a few cars in it, and there we saw Mr Elliot locking up his Rover. He came over and explained. 'They don't allow cars within the walls,' he told us, 'You can drive in to unload but then you have to park outside.'

At the suggestion of leaving his precious car exposed in a car-park after being outpaced by the Rover I really thought Walter was going to explode, and was relieved to see Mrs Elliot strolling back over the bridge. 'Ah there is Lottie,' said Elliot, and I was side-tracked from Walter's fury by this unlikely name for such an elegant creature. She came up to the car and held out her hand to me. I had not met her before. 'I am Carlotta Elliot,' she said graciously, which sounded altogether different.

At that moment the guardian of the bridge came out of the gate-house and on seeing the Delage stopped in his tracks and rubbed his eyes as if he could not believe what he saw. 'Ecco! La bella machina!' he exclaimed, rushing up to the car and bestowing a smacking kiss on the windscreen!

Before we could recover from our surprise or indeed get a word into his torrent of Italian he had produced a stick-on parking badge, given the windscreen another smacking kiss and placed the badge on the spot. 'Ecco, permesso!' he said, opening the gate with a flashing smile.

Well Jan, just imagine! The badge was to allow us to keep the car inside the walls of St Sirmione! We drove over the bridge feeling that we had been given the freedom of the city, leaving Elliot looking bemused and amused and Carlotta as near to having her mouth open as elegance would permit.

Yesterday Mr Elliot and Carlotta and I went out on the lake in a speedboat. Walter stayed behind showing off the Delage because the guardian brings a constant stream of people to look at her. Although Walter knows no Italian and the guardian little English they seem to have developed a perfect understanding, and after the triumph of being allowed to park inside the little town Walter is in heaven.

It was a cold dismal day. Our boat sped out into the middle of the lake where the boatman said hot water was gushing up from the lake bed. And sure enough when we stopped you could see bubbles coming to the surface and the water was slightly warmer to the hand than the rest of the lake which isn't nearly warm enough for bathing yet. I am longing to swim again and look forward to going on to Abano Terme where Carlotta says the swimming is delightful in the hot springs. They go there most years, she says. She seems very nice, not snooty after all. I begin to suspect she isn't English, no trace of an accent, but rather a pedantic way of forming sentences.

Our hotel is picturesque and the compact little town a gem. We eat on a vine-covered terrace, which is a bit cold in the evening to tell the truth, and above is our balcony where I am writing now in a welcome gleam of sunshine.

'The Elliots are off tomorrow, but I think I'd prefer to stay on here for a while. How do you feel, Emmie?'

'It's the most charming place, – I love it here. But won't Carlotta be disappointed if we don't go with them? She has become so attached to the Delage.'

'Yes, she has rather, hasn't she. Well perhaps we will just stay another day or so, but I don't feel inclined to be hustled about at another man's convenience.'

At Abano Terme

Dear Jan,

We had a dismal drive from Lake Garda after a cheerful send-off from St Sirmone in sunshine. Walter and the guardian parted with mutual vows of friendship and the assurance that our parking permission was eternal, and a little crowd gathered at the bridge to wish us God-speed.

But we ran into low cloud and heavy rain on the motorway to Padua. Walter put up the hood which cuts down nearly all sideways visibility, and then my windscreen-wiper failed so all I could see, mile after mile, was a continuous blurred stream of lorries through drenching spray as we overtook or were overtaken by them. They soon thundered past if Walter wasn't going fast enough. I recalled Hilaire Belloc on his Path to Rome, tramping his mile after mile in the rain in the Po valley, but all we could see of romantic places like Verona and Vicenza were huge names on exit signs.

And all the way I felt the baleful influence of Aunt Jessie's disapproval of the car being exposed to such dreadful weather. We had a snack lunch at a filling-station and towards the end of the dreary day we were relieved to see a brightening sky as we turned off the Autostrada to Padua.

But the relief was soon destroyed by Walter hearing, or imagining, a grinding noise in the back axle. It was very slight to begin with and I was numbed with travel, but by the time we limped into Abano Terme even I could hear that this was a serious, perhaps a fatal noise. At that point I did not feel we had Aunt Jessie's blessing, but I kept my thoughts to myself. We just crawled to the nearest hotel, and while Walter consulted the manager about garages I booked a room and supervised unloading the luggage.

This is an old hotel and I was brought up to a large bedroom with pale green walls and hangings in darker green. There were comfortable armchairs and the chambermaid drew back heavy curtains to reveal an odd-shaped little writing-room with great sliding windows opening on to an equally odd-shaped balcony. The effect was wonderfully soothing after such a dreadful journey.

I went out on the balcony and there below me, set in a sub-tropical garden was a huge open pool connected to another, glassed in, with a winding covered passage to the hotel. And such a smell of flowers! Genista I think. A couple were swimming in the pool and an enormously fat man was floating in the kind of ring a child would use, only huge, which looked very comical.

Tea has been sent up and I have been tempted by my own little writing-table to sit and write to you. I have been waiting for over an hour now and Walter has not yet appeared. Poor Walter, I do feel so sorry for him, – he must be totally knocked up just by the driving, and then to have a breakdown at the end of it! Luckily we have fallen into such pleasant surroundings though even I am too tired to swim tonight. The fat man is still floating in his tyre like a ship not under command, – possibly they get him out with a special hoist.

'Walter dear! Come and sit down, I will ring for more tea. Isn't this delightful?'

'I've got to go down again directly, a breakdown lorry is coming to shift the car. The back-end has seized solid now, I came to tell you.'

'But just come out on the balcony a moment. Look dear, at the garden, – and isn't the pool super?'

'You're surely not intending to dip yourself in water smelling of rotten eggs!'

'Oh Walter, don't be silly. You can't smell anything except flowers. You love swimming.'

'To make a fool of myself like that fat chap in the tyre!'

'He's probably incapacitated dear.'

'And no doubt incontinent too. The whole set-up puts me off. Anyhow we're unlikely to be here more than a day. The car will have to be entrained to Milan, or perhaps to Paris. I've no confidence in garages in this one-horse town.'

'But darling, I just booked myself a course of mud-treatments, – they won't even let you have a room unless you do...'

'Really Emmie, how can you be so frivolous with the Delage in such trouble. You'll just have to cancel. I assure you I'll be out of this place as soon as we can get away.'

Still at Abano Terme

Janice dear,

We have been here two full days and I am keeping my fingers crossed, it is so delightful. Unfortunately Walter has taken against the place, – of course he was upset by the car breaking down but luckily the garage turned out to be one which specialises in exotic cars, and I suspect they seized on the Delage as a change from tuning Mazeratis. Anyway their enthusiasm won Walter over into allowing them to take the car apart and report.

In the meanwhile I have started a course of five mud treatments, but they cannot be taken every day in case your heart conks out so it will take two weeks to complete. In fact a doctor came to my room to check up on me before beginning, and this occurred, believe it or not, at six o'clock yesterday morning. Fortunately Walter was up worrying about the car and went out to wait for the garage to open.

I was passed A1 thank goodness, and by seven o'clock was summoned to the mud-parlours in the basement, dressed in a swish white bathrobe, provided, and a shower cap. There is a special lift to the baths and pool to prevent guests splashing about on the front stairs. I told you that this is an old hotel and underground it is just like a prison. I was put to wait on a bench outside a row of cells, – there was a lot of shouting going on inside.

After a while a fierce-looking Italian woman came carrying two buckets of steaming mud and ordered me into a cell. It was all white-tiled with a number of dials on the walls, a bath in the floor with steps down, lots of hose-pipe, and a rough canvas bed. The effect was more like an experimental chamber than a health cure and very unnerving, I can tell you, at that time in the morning.

The woman ladled steaming mud from one bucket straight on to the canvas bed and invited me to remove my robe and lie on it. I climbed on meekly, the mud was boiling hot and I myself weak as a jelly about to melt. Then she plastered the other bucketful all over me and wrapped me up in thick brown paper like a parcel and finished insulating the package with extra towels. Then she looked at her watch and assuring me I'd be done in five minutes went off shutting the door behind her.

Instead of cooling down my mud seemed to be heating up, perhaps from me boiling inside. I gathered from the shouting that the fierce attendant was working to a tight schedule, running from cell to cell and plastering other women with boiling mud. It seemed I was left for hours not minutes, and I became convinced I was forgotten, missed out somehow, and would be discovered boiled to a rag if they ever found me.

At last the attendant did come back and unwrapped me. What a relief! Then she hoisted me to my feet, hosed me down with warm water and ordered me into the bath. I staggered down the steps into water which felt blissful, just the right temperature, – thank goodness they don't plunge you into cold water here or make you drink the stuff. The woman adjusted dials on the wall and bubbles came into the water, not like foam, little individual bubbles, caressing me all over. She told me it was ozone, which I doubted.

Finally she wrapped me in towels and sent me back to bed and told me to stay there until the masseuse came at eleven o'clock, – another surprise! I dozed pleasantly for a while, and I can't say I felt good for anything else as all this had been on an empty stomach, not even a cup of tea first. But when breakfast arrived I really began to enjoy myself, already feeling wonderful though a bit apprehensive about the massage, I felt I'd had enough rough treatment for one day.

The masseuse is very pleasant and speaks French, and the massage itself gentle and relaxing. The slapping and pummelling kind, she told me, is for getting fat down, and although I'd like to get rid of a few bulges I'm not going to take a chance on that for the time being.

I told her I was worried about Walter because he doesn't like the place, and goodness knows what he will do with himself with me in bed half the day if they get the car fixed. She said that husbands always get irritated unless they are having the treatment too, but I can't see Walter allowing himself to be packaged up in boiling mud.

Janice, the swimming is wonderful here in Abano! It seems unbelievable to me that one can swim outside even after dark at this time of year, the sky is such a marvellous colour, violet, velvety, filling with stars. Walter does get irritated, alas, haunts the garage by day, goes nearly demented during the long lunch break and refuses to swim in the evening. However if the place is full of husbands in an irritated state perhaps it's just as well that he has something in particular to be irritated about. But it is very sad to see him so distressed when he was so happy before. This evening they hope to tell him the extent of the damage and what can be done about it.

'Well darling, what progress?' Have they finished?'

'Really Emmie, they've only just taken the back axle down, – and of course spare parts are unobtainable. They will have to be specially made...'

'You mean in France?'

'From what I can understand the foreman is saying that the pieces can be turned out locally. But God knows if one can trust them, – and everything goes so slowly, nobody moves in the middle of the day. I don't know if I should let them take the job in hand or not...or what else I can do...'

'But darling, if we do have to stay here this hotel is very pleasant, and we shall have a chance to visit lovely places nearby.'

'How can we do that without the car?'

'They tell me the bus and train services are excellent. It is quite easy to get to Padua and on to Venice...'

'If you think I'm going to jostle with sweaty Italians to visit some rotting canals!'

'Walter, Venice is one of the wonders of the world. You'll love it, darling. What about hiring a car?'

'My dear Emmie, expenses are mounting as it is. It's bad enough being trapped in this place without gallivanting about. I simply must be around to keep an eye on things.'

Still at Abano Terme

Dear Jan,

Walter was unpersuadable as usual so I caught the bus to Padua by myself. It was a nice little bus, and you will never guess who was travelling on it, – at least I was surprised, – Mr Elliot! We knew they were here but had not got in touch with them yet. He told me that Lottie was having beauty treatment at an hotel outside Abano on alternate days from the mud, and of course she needed the car but he was glad of a change from driving anyway.

So I said I supposed he didn't see much of Carlotta and asked if he was having the mud treatment too, and he said that he seemed to grind along quite well without, but he enjoyed a swim night and morning. He seemed to accept his situation calmly. I told him what the masseuse had said about husbands getting irritable, and he smiled, – he has a nice smile, – and said he became reconciled long ago.

Then he asked what I intended to do in Padua, and I said I didn't know, and he said he had decided he had better look at the Giotto frescoes because he was ashamed of never having done so, and would I care to join him? Well I was delighted of course but when we entered the dim little chapel I was ashamed too because I didn't seem to be appreciating as I should. Then we put money into a machine and were told on earphones what to appreciate in rather peculiar English, – it didn't help much, the light was so dim, but I should have started getting educated years ago.

When we emerged into blinding sunlight Mr Elliot said he couldn't see what he was supposed to see inside and now he couldn't see at all and when he found his sunglasses he said, 'Well after that attempt to nourish my intellect I feel interested in food for the body. What do you say to a spot of lunch?' I was starving, you might imagine, and was very relieved at not having to make educated comments except agreeing that it was wonderful how the frescoes had been preserved and incredible that Giotto could paint so well before anyone else knew how. And then we found a pleasant restaurant with tables set out under a pergola with wistaria in full bloom.

What delight there is in the preliminaries of restaurant eating! Sitting down, unfolding one's napkin, deciphering the menu and consulting the wine-list! And my delight was enhanced by having the passive role. I chose canelloni to start with, which was gorgeous, and Osso bucco to follow which was a mistake, but it was blissful not to feel responsible and not to be in a hurry either. The meal took a long time and then Mr Elliot suggested taking our coffee to more comfortable chairs at the end of the terrace.

We sat very quietly and I was about to remark on the scent of the wistaria when I noticed that Mr Elliot was drifting off to sleep. Which must be infectious during siesta time because the next I knew was waking up to find Mr Elliot looking down on me with an amused expression. I felt very embarrassed. 'You have been having a little nap, Emmie,' he said, 'and as a matter of fact I had one too, – I hope I wasn't snoring.' And I said I hoped I didn't have my mouth open, and he said I looked very charming, which I doubt, and then suggested we go back into Padua to wake ourselves up with tea in the famous 'Café without doors'.

We drove back in a taxi and Mr Elliot told me that the Pedrochi Café had been built about 1830 opposite Padua University and was designed without doors for easy access. He said the last time he was there the students were having a rag, dressed up and actually drinking out of their distinctive hats which have curled brims extending in front into a sort of snout about a foot long. –and they had filled these curled brims with wine and were drinking from the snouts! He was enjoying this spectacle when he noticed that the waiters were very uneasy and then positively fearful as the students became more rowdy. He said the place eventually had to be cleared by the police, who were luckily very good-humoured on that occasion, as ready to join in the fun as to give anyone a crack on the head, – so the students were expelled with no more damage than a few glasses broken, and then the doors were shut. Because there are doors now, Mr Elliot said, huge iron-fretted glass doors, usually kept open.

In the city's narrow streets our taxi came up behind a Range Rover filled with Scotsmen in full Highland rig, which was surprising. The traffic was so slow Mr Elliot said we might as well walk, which we did and found that the streets were crowded with elderly men in Tyrolean dress, leather shorts, brief jackets and green felt hats with little feathers. As this is not a climbing area we wondered what they were doing, and some were in the 'Café Without Doors' when we reached it.

Janice, – how to describe this strange glamorous place? It is still entirely open with three huge doorways opening from the squares into three rooms, one red, one green, one white. There are plush banquettes and chairs, and wrought-iron tables. Gold-framed mirrors line the walls reflecting the counters and the scene of a lost world We strolled through the rooms in which any melancholy of temps perdu was today replaced by the cheerfulness of the mountain men who were drinking a clear red liquid, steaming hot, out of the tiniest glass tea-cups and saucers. A most incongruous sight! There was still plenty of room so we sat down on a velvet banquette and Mr Elliot asked if I would like tea but I said I simply must try the steaming red drink which looked so pretty in the little glass tea-cups.

More mountaineers were thronging in, – they were all kissing and embracing each other but with a definite sense of hierarchy. We wondered if the different sprigs of feathers in their hats denoted rank. We got rather squashed up on our banquette, and then we noticed the Scots arriving at the far end. They made a splendid show coming in – with the swing of their kilts and the poise of their heads, but we didn't see anybody attempting to kiss them, and soon they were lost to view.

Our drinks arrived and what a shock when I tried to drink, – the steam was so potent I couldn't get near the liquid! Every approach was like a stiff dose of the smelling-salts which my grandmother used when I was a child. Only this sniff was much jollier, alcoholic, and made me laugh. The men of the mountains were knocking theirs back boiling hot and calling for more, so I tried again and still choked before I could get my mouth to it. Mr Elliot was very amused and said he would let his cool down first, which I told him was cheating.

A nice French woman, separated from her husband by the crowd, was squashed up next to us and inclined to be chatty. She told us that we had chanced on a rassemblement of highland troops who had fought side by side and even each other during the war. She explained that they felt an affinity, even when fighting, whichever side they were on. Men from all sides of the Alps, the Highlands of Scotland and further afield had gathered together with the mountains in common. Her brother had been killed by an Italian, she said, and yet she had come. This touching story, so chivalrous, so sad, gave a strange extra dimension to our glamorous surroundings.

We journeyed back to Abano in the little bus and wondered how the Delage was progressing. I told Mr Elliot about

Walter's confidence in Aunt Jessie's blessing on his inheritance, but that I suspected that the car had been so carefully maintained rather as a memorial to Uncle Albert than a legacy to Walter, – and how this sometimes made me uneasy. Mr Elliot laughed and christened the Delage the Albert Memorial, which made me laugh too, but thinking of car trouble made me wish we could drive on in the little bus for ever.

Now I am back at my writing-table and very concerned because Walter isn't in yet. He was very put out when I went off alone this morning, – said I was abandoning him. But Janice, the day has been magical, and my feelings are still revelling! I don't want to talk of it to anyone else, but I have loved writing it all down for you. Could you keep this letter and give it back to me sometime?

'Walter! What happened to you? I've been quite worried.'

'I'm fine, darling. Did you enjoy your day?'

'Yes, I met Mr Elliot on the bus…'

'Poor darling! That's what comes of catching buses. Just as well I didn't go…'

'It was very pleasant, we…'

'…because by a happy chance I encountered Mrs Elliot, – and got myself properly ticked off for not reporting our arrival! I explained about the Delage breaking down, – and you know, Emmie, she seemed genuinely hurt. She said I should have gone to her for help immediately…'

'Carlotta Elliot help with a motor-car!'

'Oh don't be silly dear. Because she speaks Italian of course. I was still puzzled about what was going on so she insisted on driving me back to the garage, – that's why I'm delayed. They were just shutting up, but didn't mind stopping to talk when they saw her. In fact they were quite impressed, – and now I come to think of it, probably took her for you since you've never bothered to show your face there yet.'

'Much good I could do if I did!'

'Anyway what they told her was very reassuring, – it seems the parts are just being put in hand, – to be turned out by a local engineering firm. I was so grateful for her help that when she invited us to their hotel for dinner tomorrow evening I could hardly refuse, could I. So what do you say, darling?'

'It sounds delightful to me.'

'We are asked to come in time for a swim in their pool first, before drinks. That seems to be the drill here.'

Abano Terme

Dearest Janice,

I haven't put pen to paper for quite a while because recent events have certainly modified our life-style. Dear me, – is that a journalistic cliché? I'm never sure what's what as they fly out. Luckily I am only writing for you, – to forgive or admire as appropriate.

The thing is that we have fallen into the cheerful habit of having dinner with the Elliots, either in their hotel or ours. And I must say Carlotta is very nice and has been so helpful to Walter, – acting as interpreter at the garage, which is real kindness as it must be very tedious. On the first evening she invited us to their hotel which also has its own hot springs and an open swimming-pool in a garden, surrounded by a terrace set about with fragments of dug-up Roman statues and lovely trees and shrubs.

And Walter actually swam! I was so glad, it was just what he needed and has made him much more cheerful. He still looks very well in bathing-trunks and I could see him eyeing my poor Mr Elliot who has rather a pot. Then we had drinks and I felt wonderfully relaxed and happy after the swimming and all the soins du corps of the morning, which really do one good, I can tell you. Mr Elliot was sitting next to me and appeared happy too, though quiet. I think he is simply a contented kind of man.

Actually there was a lot to talk about. Carlotta knows so much about the Roman remains, and besides she wanted to hear every detail of our adventures on the road, so somehow there was no opportunity for anyone to be interested in what Mr Elliot and I were doing the day before, rather to my relief.

Their hotel has better food than ours which is rather stodgy. Carlotta doesn't seem to mind as she eats very little, – but I feel so hungry it is difficult to cut down. On the other hand our pool is more pleasant on cool evenings because it is partly covered, you can swim in and out under a plastic flap. Inside the source gushing from several outlets is really hot but of course the outer pool is cooler though still warm and it is fascinating to dive under the flap out of the warm lighted building and come up under a darkening sky, violet, velvety, filling with stars –but I think I told you this before.

While writing your letter has arrived. Very welcome! It seems you have received mine safely in spite of strikes. Your gossip about Oxford seem to come from another world and I have difficulty bringing my wits to bear. But the delays with your volume and The Press! Whatever next! I haven't the faintest idea what you mean about Alec being preoccupied with the philosophical implications of the 'Fifth generation'. Still it's good to hear he has something to take his mind off Horace.

Walter is still reluctant to travel on buses and I haven't pressed him again because I always hope that Mr Elliot will be on the bus, – and so far he always has been. He is an expert on where to go and how to get there. I wanted to see Romeo and Julliet's Verona and he took me. It was another blissful day, – though except for the distinctive battlements of the Montagues and Capulets I found the town rather disappointing, and Juliet's dismal little balcony didn't come anywhere near my romantic expectation. On the other hand whereas in a theatre the play always seemed just a story, in Verona I really began to believe in it. The townspeople certainly do.

'Sorry to have kept your husband so late, Emma, you will think I've been leading him astray. Move up, Sidney, and let me sit down. That's better. So what did you do with your day, Emma?'

'I…we were just in Padua, it was very nice…'

'Well today I felt an absolute need for intellectual refreshment, and I said to myself 'Enough of this preoccupation with the body.' So when I rang Walter as usual to see if he needed my voice at the garage, I suggested that he should come with me to visit the Capella degli Scrovegni…'

'The Giotto frescoes!'

'Ah yes, – the masterpieces of my beloved Ambrogiotto di Bondone! I go to see them whenever we are here, and each time I enter that dim hallowed place I am struck again by the freshness of the paintings, – their innocence, – but obviously you are familiar with them?'

'Well I've only listened to the tapes, – when we were there...'

'Oh the tapes! I never listen to anything that might distract my eyes, – and I give conducted parties a wide berth for the same reason. I need only look to feel my intellect refreshed, – my very soul nourished. Walter was very impressed.'

'He was!'

'Lottie my dear, we've already had our swim and a drink.

I'm sure Emmie is hungry. What we're all in need of now is nourishment for our bodies. So I suggest we go in. Or do you want to swim, Walter?'

'I must admit to feeling rather peckish.'

'How these men bully us, Emma. Well as I eat very little I can swim later in the evening.'

'So you've all decided then? Let me see, – I think I will have the green tagliattelli first, and then the ham stuffed with cheese, – and then...'

'Sidney, for goodness sake! Can't you see you are putting on weight?'

'I'm only having the same as Walter.'

'Walter has a different metabolism, he can eat what he likes...'

'Whereas I have somewhere to put it! And Emmie is having canelloni yet again...'

'It suits Emma to be a little plump.'

'I agree with you there, darling! What do we drink with it, Walter?'

'You haven't finished telling me about your Delage, Carlotta. I'm sure Emmie would like to hear...'

'The end was such a sad story, Walter, I can hardly bear to dwell on it.'

'Walter tells me the car belonged to your grandfather?'

'Yes, Emma, and when he died she was laid up in our old stable. Of course old cars were not of any value then so nobody took much notice when we children found her a fascinating place to play house in. She seemed huge to me, with enormous soft seats covered in fawn cloth. There was a sliding window separating front from back and a speaking-tube, and blinds to pull up and down, and crystal flower vases and little cupboards to keep treasures in. You can imagine how much we loved it. But of course we grew out of that stage, mice nested in the upholstery and the tyres went flat and nobody cared much. I remember my father saying he would like to restore her but that he could hardly keep our roof in repair with me at boarding school and my brother at University.

'Then, one winter when I was about fifteen and my father was away in Hong-Kong, there was a terrible storm, the roof of the stable was blown in and a wall collapsed on the Delage. I've never seen such a disaster. My mother was in despair until she found that the insurance would pay for the new building and she got the work put in hand at once. The car hadn't been insured for years and the demolition people just dug into the rubble and took the whole lot away. My father was furious when he came home to find a new building but no car. And I wept. I still weep now when I think of it, I assure you I positively weep. You can feel for me, Walter.'

'Indeed I can, Carlotta!'

'As I remember, Lottie, you have always said you were delighted to have the stable for your pony.'

'That is of course, Sidney, and has nothing to do with my feelings for the car. Walter understands...'

'Yes, and I'm beginning to see the folly of using the Delage for touring. She is really a museum piece. I intend putting her on the car-train home.'

Abano Terme

Janice dear,

This is probably the last letter I shall write from here, alas. My cure is finished, not the vestige of an ache left, – but that of course is incidental, – the car repairs are being completed today. Walter has just gone over to the Elliot's hotel as Carlotta has promised to take him to the garage.

I'm afraid your prediction of my becoming a 'vintage car widow' will soon be only too true. Walter now realises that the Delage is too precious to tour about in and says he will never take her out of England again. Well we have had this tour at least, the experience of my lifetime, and out of many memorable days yesterday was the best yet.

I went out for the early bus and wondered if Mr Elliot would be there. I know it sounds silly not to make any forward arrangement, but I think if we did it would mean mentioning it in advance, whereas if we meet by chance there is no need, and usually no opportunity to say anything. . Anyway there was Mr Elliot already waiting at the bus-stop, sitting on a bench and trying to read La Stampa, but not doing very well, he said, because with Lottie being so educated he hardly ever has to use his brain.

I asked if Carlotta was part Italian, and he told me she is as English as you or me (-I?) and was christened Charlotte and didn't like it, but he was used to calling her Lottie and wasn't going to change, but he did sympathise with her because he hated being called Sidney, which was a name you could do nothing with to make it sound any better, and people were reluctant to use it. He noticed I didn't call him anything whereas Emmie was charming and very chummy. I felt myself blushing, – at my age! Because it is quite true, he will always seem like Mr Elliot to me.

The bus came and Mr Elliot said that as we were early and the weather just right we should take the train from Padua to Venice. Well since you know Venice, Jan, I need hardly write more, especially as we just pottered about soaking up the feel of the place, and I was surprised at the wonderful fresh air and smell of the sea because the weather was just right with the wind in the right direction, as Mr Elliot had predicted. We had coffee at Florian's in St Mark's Square, sitting inside to appreciate the atmosphere, but by then I was intoxicated with atmosphere and would have been quite lost as we continued strolling round the intricate network of canals and little bridges. We were both pretty flopped out as we came on to the Grand Canal near the Rialto and sat down to have a drink and some lunch.

Although we lingered over the meal we were still a bit footsore and not inclined to be energetic so Mr Elliot said we must treat ourselves to a gondola for the afternoon when the squares get more crowded. I dread to think what it must have cost but it was like a dream gliding round the deserted canals in siesta time and I'm not sure the gondolier wasn't having his siesta standing up. He rowed so quietly, so gently, blending the rhythm of Offenbach's barcarole in my head with the motion of the boat and water lapping against weedy crumbling walls, – sucking in and out of gratings under foliage tumbling from neglected gardens. The ripples were smooth as a sucked sweet and in shafts of sunlight soft glittering balls of light bounced gently from one hollow to another like a trick of camera. Mr Elliot said that next year we must visit the islands and I said I was afraid that for me there could not be a next year and he sighed

'Walter! Are you back so soon? Isn't the car ready?'

'We haven't started yet, darling. Carlotta suggested that it would be polite to have a drink with the mechanics. She wants you to come too…'

'How nice, I'll just comb my hair…'

'Don't bother about that, – you look alright. Carlotta and Elliot are waiting in the car, – we can't keep them hanging about. Oh do hurry up, Emmie!'

Well Jan, I had to break off because Walter came to fetch me to have a drink with the mechanics who have worked such wonders with the car.

It was Carlotta's idea, – she drove the Rover with Walter sitting next to her and Mr Elliot and I sitting in the back, – and when we reached the garage an astonishing sight met our eyes. There was the Delage ready, all polished and gleaming and beside it a table covered with a white cloth and laid out with glasses and a magnum of Champagne in an ice-bucket. It had all been laid out with Carlotta's own hand as a surprise for Walter! And standing by were the mechanics all scrubbed up in clean shirts with the foreman who carried flowers.

But the car! You have probably forgotten me mentioning that its long bonnet is strapped down with a hefty leather belt which seems to have been a feature of sports cars of that era and which had vastly intrigued Carlotta. I'd heard her joking with Walter, saying that the leather belt was a mere male symbol because their Delage had a bonnet just as long which did not need strapping down.

So to tease Walter Carlotta had actually dressed the car for the party by concealing the belt with a wide white satin ribbon which she had tied in a huge bow on top. Well this is the kind of charming witty gesture absolutely typical of Carlotta. The kind of little joke which would never have entered my mind, – and probably would not have gone down very well if it had.

But Walter was enchanted. He let out a gasp of delight, and as he and Carlotta got out of the Rover the foreman came over and presented them with flowers, a little spray for her and a buttonhole for Walter. This was the mechanics' idea and a surprise for Carlotta who also gave an exclamation of delight. Mr Elliot and I got out of the back of the Rover like a pair of guests and of course Carlotta tried to pass the flowers to me, and no doubt the foreman thought she was being polite, and of course I pressed them back on her. She certainly deserved them, – for being so helpful, and organising such a delightful party..

There was a cheerful bang as the Champagne cork flew out, – in fact it turned out to be Asti Spumante, more suitable for the occasion. And the mechanics, pouring out and handing glasses were so easy and charming it hardly mattered that Carlotta was the only interpreter, she managed so well.

Jokes flashed back and forth somehow seeming funnier when only partly understood and we all began to feel very witty. Another pouring of drink went round and Walter told them to steady on there because he could not drink and drive, and everyone laughed at the suggestion that anybody could get tipsy on two glasses of Asti Spumante. But I could for one, and I did.

On the third topping up Walter shouted 'Quiet everyone! Basta, basta!' and lifted his glass for toasts. We drank to the mechanics who had done so well, and then to the foreman, and to Carlotta for being interpreter, – obviously there had been more bottles lurking in reserve, and then on the last round Walter lifted his glass and said, 'Here's to next year in Abano Terme!' Carlotta translated, and really Jan, I could hardly believe my ears in either language.

Well to keep you out of suspense, Walter did get back safely to the hotel, though I felt apprehensive when he was prepared to drive with the great satin bow in situ. But Carlotta would not let him. She removed it with her own hands and said that for all its strident masculinity she had taken a particular liking to this Delage. And then she kissed the windscreen on the spot where the permesso of St Sirmione was still displayed, and two mechanics opened the car doors and Walter climbed into the driving-seat and Carlotta folded herself gracefully into the other. I think by then she had quite forgotten that perhaps that place was mine.

But I was entirely content when my Mr Elliot, imitating the Italians, opened the Rover door for me with an exaggerated flourish. We both giggled, and as he drove me back the Asti Spumante was still swirling deliciously in my brain, together with Walter's magic words. 'Here's to next year in Abano Terme.'

CARLOTTA IN OXFORD

'Janice, it's me, – to give you our Woodstock number, it's a private house...'

'How soon do you go there, Emmie?' I forget when the Rally takes place.'

'Really Janice! I've kept telling you! The Rally is in Blenheim Park, – tomorrow and we are already there, – here I mean. Walter decided to come two days early because they have a good garage, – and it's been a nerve-wracking job, I can tell you, preparing for a Concours d'Elegance...'

'For God's sake, Emmie, don't go on about that damned car again. Can't you amuse me with some romantic flutters?'

'Well, by an odd chance it is connected, Jan. That's what I really wanted to tell...'

'My dear Emmie, I am all ears!'

'Well Carlotta telephoned one morning when I was out, – I always seem to miss her, but never mind. I think I told you they were abroad all summer, but you will never guess what! Walter tells me that they will be here in Woodstock for the Rally. Isn't it extraordinary?'

'Extraordinary?'

'Well I think it is, and what's more they will be putting up at The Bear, which we couldn't afford anyway, and how they managed it I can't imagine, – so many rich people are exhibiting their cars we heard you couldn't get a room there for love or money!'

'And was it for love in the case of your Elliots, Emmie?'

'Oh Janice, what do you think? My heart did skip a beat when Walter told me.'

'You are not telling me your heart is still at risk!

'Worse than ever it seems, – I know you think I'm stupid, – and I'm so afraid of it showing.'

'But Walter must be pretty occupied.'

'Oh I don't mean Walter, he'd never notice, and these past weeks have been an awful strain, getting the car into tip-top condition, and driving here, – he is looking quite worn out. No Jan, I am worried about Carlotta, – she is really very nice, I've told you, and so kind. And yet I did have this feeling that...well...'

'That your Mr Elliot feels as you do?'

'Not so foolishly, I'm sure. But still –I did feel there was something...Oh dear, Walter is calling. Back to the polishing, I'm afraid...'

'Goodbye then, Emmie, – but do keep in touch. I shall look forward to the next instalment.'

'Walter! You've made her positively dazzling! She looks perfect to me.'

'Well dear, no doubt the judges will have a more critical eye. But you can help by inspecting from all angles. Only for goodness sake! What's the use asking you to help if you're going to make finger marks!'

'I'm not, I was just rubbing a smudge with a clean handkerchief. But what will you do if it rains, Walter? The car will be splashed all over before we get into the Park.'

'Why does everything you say have to be negative? And be specially careful there with the lamps... Elliot! My dear fellow, how nice to see you here! And Carlotta, Benvenuto!'

'Emma, Walter! How lovely to see you both. We have just now arrived. But first of all let me look at my favourite car. The second love of my life, I assure you. Walter, she is positively dazzling!'

'So I was just telling him, Carlotta. But don't dare to kiss her, Walter doesn't allow smudges.'

'Emma! Don't tell me has cleaned off the kisses! Can he have forgotten so soon? Our darling Guardian of the bridge? But no, I see he has left the permesso. Ever the practical man. I must look all round with the eyes of a judge... My dear Walter, you have excelled yourself!'

'You think we might at least get a mention?'

'I haven't a doubt about it. My dears, how exciting all this is! You've no idea how lovely it is to be back in England. I've never visited Blenheim Palace before, and the autumn colours are splendid. We must pray for a fine day.'

'The forecast is set fair, for what that's worth. But don't you think the leather has come up well? And just look round here on the other side...'

'So how is Emmie? Looking somewhat peaky, I fear. Have you been neglecting yourself?'

'I'm fine, really, though it has been a bit of a strain, preparing the car. Not that I actually do much. Poor Walter is quite fagged out...'

'He looks sprightly enough to me at the moment. Well Emmie, we must think of some nice treats to put back the bloom in your cheeks, and plump you up like you were in Abano.'

'...so you will be looking in on the show, tomorrow, Carlotta?'

'Nothing could keep me away.'

'We are to have the cars on display all morning, and the parade is in the afternoon.'

'Then if you will allow us to 'assist' in the French sense of the word, we will spend the day with you.'

'I think, Lottie, we might put up a picnic for our exhibitors. If I know anything of these affairs they will be much too pressed to think of eating.'

'Yes, Sidney, that was exactly my intention. Unless you have other plans for food, Emma?'

'Not really, I was just going to nip out to the shops...'

'My dear, don't give it another thought. I will organise everything.'

'Oxford 98245'

'Am I disturbing you Jan? Nobody is awake here yet, and as you're such an early riser I thought we could have a quiet chat...'

'Nothing could be better timed, Emmie. The Sunday papers haven't arrived yet and I'm just back in bed with a pot of coffee beside me.'

'You didn't come to look at the cars yesterday, and it was quite an experience I can tell you...'

'I dare say it was dear, but not my sort of thing, as you know. I was glad to see you had fine weather. Did your friends turn up?'

'Yes they came the day before...'

'And how does your Mr Elliot stand up to a second look? Or was it just a shipboard romance?'

'Not for me at least, but on his side I hardly dare to guess. He seems to be naturally kind...'

'Ah! But does his wife find him so?'

'Well he teases her, and Carlotta hen-pecks a bit, but then she has such a capacity for enjoyment, – she makes life seem such fun.'

'And did Walter's car win a prize?'

'Not quite, but he got a sort of honourable mention which made him very happy.'

'So it was worth all the fret and worry?'

'Indeed it was, and anyway once we had driven into the Park and found our allotted places Walter was a changed being. There was an infectious feeling of camaraderie besides the rivalry, – which infected me too. And the cars were really fabulous. The veteran Rolls were lined up next to us and standing alongside the Delage was the most picturesque Rolls Royce you could imagine. Open, very high at the back and yards long, – with brass fittings all over and a convoluted brass horn.

'It belonged to an old, old man who was polishing brass all morning with a young helper. He told me the brass goes off in no time. Of course Walter was busy polishing too and very cheerful, and I helped by removing leaves which occasionally fell on the cars. The autumn colours were fantastic and Blenheim Palace looked splendid in the sunshine.'

'Weren't your friends with you?'

'Yes, they arrived about eleven o'clock and unloaded a huge hamper and cold-box with tables and chairs, – Carlotta had thought of everything. Then she stayed with us while Mr Elliot went to park the car. Carlotta was wearing a gorgeous 1930'ish dress and hat, – nothing ludicrous or fancy-dress, – she could have worn it anywhere, but period enough to make people think she belonged to the Delage when the public was let in to view the cars.'

'How did you take to being on show?'

'Don't dare to be snooty, Janice, it was lovely. Though to tell the truth I felt so shy when people first came past I hid myself behind the Rolls. But everyone was so interested I was soon tempted out to listen to the old man relating the history of his car. The car seemed to have been an historical exhibit even in his living memory and he was very proud of all the prizes he had won. By that time Mr Elliot was listening too, having come back from parking his car, – quite two miles off, he said, which I didn't believe.

'In the meanwhile Walter was showing the engine of the Delage to a couple of young enthusiasts. He had unstrapped the leather belt and they all had their heads inside the bonnet. Carlotta was seated inside the car and Mr Elliot called, 'Have you had a breakdown, Lottie?' making me laugh because that was just what it looked like. Carlotta said she would probably have been more suitably dressed in white dungarees, and Walter took his head out of the engine and said, just wait till the judges saw her in the Concours d'élegance, and if the car won a prize it would be due to her. The young men shouted, 'Hear, hear' and then went back to the technicalities...'

'Never mind that, Em, tell me what the Elliots brought to eat.'

'My dear, you'd never believe what was unpacked, with a Champagne bucket and real Champagne this time. The owner of the Rolls had been abandoned by his helper and was sitting very disconsolate on his running-board holding a small sandwich bag. Carlotta invited him to join us, which he did, grumbling at spectators who envied his car but had no idea what hard work it was maintaining it. An all year round job, he said, and before shows he was working eighteen hours a day. Of course Walter was only to ready to agree so Carlotta tried soothing them with Champagne, which made the old mad feel even more sad and neglected, saying that his wife gave up coming to rallies years ago, – in the end we gagged him with food...'

'I suppose, Emmie you will soon get fed-up with these male games?'

'Goodness, I was already fed-up this time, earlier on, with all the fuss. But just think what I would have missed, Jan, missing this one...'

'You mean missing your Mr Elliot?'

'It doesn't bear thinking about. And besides we had such a lovely time once Walter relaxed, sitting in the sun, drinking Champagne and eating delicious food, thanks to Carlotta. Just as well I wasn't competing or my efforts would have been put to shame. Everything tasted so good, – smoked salmon with bread and butter to start with and then roast chicken, ham and salad, all more than we could eat, and a heavenly Stilton, and ice-cream. I can't tell you how delicious it all was...'

'But you are telling me, and making me regret I didn't buy a ticket at the gate to join you for the meal, – I could have brought Alec, to save cooking,'

'And I'll tell you what. I especially enjoyed that people were still passing, and envying us. I enjoyed every minute. So there! I must admit though to mentally keeping my fingers crossed hoping that we really do have Aunt Jessie's blessing which Walter so firmly believes in, and I can't help doubting.'

'However did you keep awake in the afternoon?'

'Well we were aroused to the business of the day when the old man's helper came back all togged up in chauffeur's uniform, dark green to match the car, leggings, brass buttons, very handsome, just like in a film. The old man who had dozed off was woken up and went round his brass again and then the chauffeur helped him up into the high back seat and they were ready.'

Of course Walter invited Mr Elliot and Carlotta to drive in the Delage, but Mr Elliot said he must decline because he wasn't dressed for it, which made me realise that I wasn't dressed for it either and besides I hadn't finished clearing up the food. So we all persuaded Carlotta that she would represent us best and eventually they drove off, Walter very happy, and Carlotta, I must say, the nicest garnish the Delage could possible have.'

'While you had your paramour to yourself for the afternoon. Cunning creature!'

'Oh Jan, you can't imagine how relaxing it was after all that excitement. Obviously I expected to watch the parade but Mr Elliot said a walk in the Park would be much more pleasant, and shake down our lunch. But I said how could we leave the picnic gear unguarded? And two women on the other side, still sitting in their clutter, overheard and said that they didn't intend to stir for anything except to brew up a cup of tea, and they would keep a eye on our gear to make sure no villains made off with it. So we wandered away beyond the crowds and ended by sitting quietly near the edge of the lake...'

'Just as well I didn't come.'

'I dare say an afternoon like that might bore you but it was sheer bliss to me. Then we went into the town and had some tea which made us quite late but when we got back there was no need to apologise because Carlotta and Walter were so excited about their honourable mention. They told us that the old man had fallen sound asleep again in the back of the Rolls Royce and had to be woken up to receive his prize. It was such a relief, and I felt overflowing with happiness, – but I am so afraid, Jan, that sooner or later my feelings will show…'

'It looks to me, dear, that you could hardly be in circumstances more favourable to deception. Ah, there's the front door, it must be Cedric putting in our Sunday papers, – and Alec is moving, – so I suppose I'd better get myself up and show willing and boil him an egg.'

'The Elliots have invited us to dinner at The Bear tomorrow evening.'

'But Walter, – we owe them already for the picnic!'

'Yes it is embarrassing, – but Carlotta was so insistent, – the menu is specially chosen, she said, – it seemed churlish to refuse…'

'But how can we return their hospitality when we are only here for one more day?'

'Well that is what I want to suggest, dear. Carlotta would like to see more of Oxford while they are here. So I was thinking we might stay on for a few days too, – there is no trouble about our accommodation, I've checked. What do you say, darling?'

'It sounds delightful to me, and I've been longing to see Janice…'

'That is rather what I am hoping. I thought with your Oxford connection we might be able to make some return to the Elliots by showing them places where ordinary tourists aren't allowed. Carlotta seems to think Alec's college is of particular interest…'

'Yes, I talked of it in Abano. I'm sure that Janice will be glad to show them interesting parts of Oxford.'

'Well dear, a don's wife isn't quite the same as a don, and Carlotta has taken so much trouble I was hoping that Alec might exercise himself, – though God knows he's a dull dog…'

'Walter! Janice is an historian in her own right, – and Alec is a distinguished scholar, – he only missed becoming Master by a hair's breadth…'

'Exactly my point, a second class brain if ever I met one. These chaps get a Fellowship early and then expect to live on that success for the rest of their lives…'

'Really Walter! Sometimes I think you are jealous!'

'Nothing to be jealous of, dear. I'm sure Alec is an excellent chap in his way, and after all Janice is your oldest friend...'

'Indeed she is. I am sure she will do all she can to help, and I'd be glad to ask her. But I wouldn't dream of presuming on our friendship to suggest that she should bother Alec.'

'Impossible for the next few days I'm afraid, Emmie. I'm tied up with this wretched seminar, as our American visitors call it, – I told you...'

'Oh yes, so you did, I'd quite forgotten.'

'I would love to meet your Mr Elliot and Carlotta, but the evenings too...'

'As a matter of fact, Jan, – I hardly dare to suggest this, – Walter was hoping that perhaps Alec might...'

'My dear, Alec is so preoccupied with his 'Fifth generation' he doesn't even exchange a word with me.'

'You keep talking of this fifth generation, but whatever does it mean?'

'Why it's a future generation of computers, Emmie, computers which will learn for themselves, as far as I can gather, and be able to teach, and probably be able to think for themselves, I shouldn't wonder. Alec says that the philosophical implications are staggering, – you can imagine...'

'Good heavens, Jan, indeed I can. But I can't imagine Alec dabbling in computers!'

'Alec doesn't dabble, dear.'

'Sorry Jan, I'm sure he doesn't, – but you said he was quite baffled by the computer you gave him for his birthday...'

'Oh that's just at the technical level, Emmie, and has nothing to do with the philosophy of the subject. I don't know a thing about computers either but I understand that the men on the ground haven't even got their third generation worked out yet so no doubt Alec will have time to master his toy before they catch up with him. If philosophers are to do any good they have to be an advance guard, you know...'

'Goodness, no wonder Alec is preoccupied.'

'Well Emmie, he feels that if only he can seize its essence this is going to be his great work at last...'

'Janice, please don't think of disturbing him on our account.'

'I don't know, Emmie, I am just thinking. I don't see why Alec shouldn't be disturbed once in a while, – or why I should be the one who is expected to do the chores and running about. His mother is coming to stay next week, and she is not my favourite person, as you know, – nor Alec's either for that matter. So he will feel he owes me, – and there is nothing like getting paid in advance, is there? I will try a little blackmail, Emmie, and let you know.'

'You're surely not asking me to parade a gaggle of silly women around College, – it's out of the question!'

'They are not silly women, Alec, and this is a mixed party of four.'

'But it's the women who make the cackle. –and you know how Horace hates my guests…'

'My dear Alec, you simply must get over this paranoia about Horace…'

'It is no paranoia I assure you, – even the Fellows who voted him in have begun to feel the same. All that interests him now is chairing every blessed committee they think up, or fidgeting over his precious garden.'

'The College garden is unique, Alec, of course he should be proud of it. Still, if you can't be bothered with my friends I will have to do the best I can. Only Friday is my first free day, – which means you will have to go to London to meet your mother's train. She says she needs to go to Harrods to change some tea-towels, – she will be glad of your support if there's any problem, and you can give her lunch there. Afterwards she plans to look round C&A at Oxford Circus, which will be quite easy if you take a taxi…'

'But didn't you say your friends wanted to visit Oxford tomorrow? I could give them a tour of Bodley, with my key, I suppose, – the Camera and the underground passage, – which always impresses people, – and they'd have to be quiet. I'll have a word with the Secretary. But I draw the line at College, – Horace…'

'Oh for God's sake Alec, stop going on about Horace.'

'I've fixed it Emmie. Not College I am afraid. The usual problem about Horace, – but Alec will show you all the places in Bodley where ordinary mortals aren't allowed.'

'What a pretty dining-room this is Carlotta. We haven't dined here before.'

'Yes Emma, we find the atmosphere pleasing, and they look after us very well. How is your trout, Walter?'

'Delicious, Carlotta.'

'They get it fresh from a trout farm every day.

'And the wine, Elliot, an excellent choice.'

'Janice is so sorry to miss meeting you, Carlotta, but she is tied up with some sort of Seminar…'

'On Interdisciplinary studies, I am told. Her husband is a philosopher, is he not?'

'Yes, and he is very occupied too at the moment, writing about a fifth generation of computers which Janice says will be able to learn and think and everything, – only that they haven't been invented yet. But they will be, and Janice says that philosophers have to figure out the future, ahead of developments, – not just the past, – which was certainly a surprise to me…'

'How very interesting, and how kind of him to give up his time in the circumstances.'

'Yes, it's a pity he can't show you his college, for some reason I don't understand. But Janice says we'll find the Bodleian Library fascinating.'

'Good grief, Lottie, so all your research on the college goes to waste, – you will have to swat up Bodley instead!'

'Information is never wasted, Sidney. One informs oneself as a matter of course, – at least I do.'

'Well my love, you certainly deserve full marks for your use of information.'

'Sidney, you are neglecting Walter, – he needs some more wine. But now, Walter, you must tell me what plans you have for showing the Delage next…'

'You are looking very pretty tonight, Emmie.'

'It's the lighting I expect, – these lovely soft lampshades, – and everyone seems so cheerful, I feel so relaxed somehow, – and happy.'

'Yes, it's a nice pub, – and it's good to see you happy, Emmie. I am glad you and Walter decided to stay on. We are in for another intellectual feast tomorrow it seems.'

'Oxford 98245'

'Janice! My dear we are so grateful to Alec for giving us such a wonderful tour. Carlotta was fascinated, – he made it all so interesting.'

'Alec is always at his best imparting information.'

'Yes, he was perfectly sweet, but unfortunately Walter was not at his best. Perhaps it was delayed reaction after the Rally, he got really worn out, you know. I do hope Alec didn't notice, or feel hurt...'

'On the contrary, Emmie, Alec thoroughly enjoyed himself. In fact I've never seen such a change come over anyone, – he arrived home like a dog with two tails, and was humming to himself all evening. I am consumed with curiosity. You must give me a blow by blow account of how the tour went.'

'Well, we met Alec in the hall of the New Bodleian which is pretty dismal, as you know. But he took us up in a lift directly to the top of the building and into a red-carpeted reading-room with huge windows and a panorama of all the towers and spires of Oxford which fairly took my breath away...'

'I understand your Mrs Elliot found it spiritually uplifting.'

'Yes, I heard Carlotta exclaim, which made Alec lower his voice to remind us of the readers, so from then on we were quiet as mice while he whispered which college was which and all the landmarks. Then he led us through a locked door at the back and we found ourselves among tiers and tiers of books in unreadable scripts. Alec told us we were on the top floor of the book-stack, and on the further side we came to narrow windows looking over a sea of trees which Alec said were the gardens of Trinity and St Johns, and the autumn colours were marvellous...'

'Yes, yes, Emmie, I do know the geography of the place, no need to describe the flora, – I am interested in your particular fauna.'

'Really Janice, you are exasperating. You ask me for a blow by blow account and then don't let me tell you what we saw!'

'Sorry dear, I'll try to pipe down.'

'Well then we got into another tiny lift which was supposed to carry seven people but was jam-packed with the five of us, and we went down, down, down into the bowels of the earth. Eleven floors, Alec said, and we were rather jolly being squashed up because we were able to talk out loud. In fact we even had to shout when we got out there was such a clatter of machinery which Alec told us was the famous conveyor which carries books to and from the book-stack to all the reading-rooms. Then he led us around more shelves to a huge caged-in structure where the conveyor was ejecting and loading boxes of books, – but you know all about that too. Mr Elliot said Jules Verne and Heath Robinson must have put their heads together to invent it. Also you know that tube running alongside, which makes sucking noises at the outlet, and suddenly a capsule flew out and a girl came an opened it and found a message inside.

'Carlotta exclaimed, 'A p-neumatique!' She said there used to be a system like that in Paris and one could post messages in it all over the city. Alec said Carlotta couldn't possibly be old enough to remember that, and Carlotta replied that her grandmother had told her about it....'

'The tour is coming to life. Go on Emmie.'

'Well then Alec took us into the tunnel which runs under Broad Street and climbs quite steeply uphill. The conveyor was chuntering along beside us carrying its boxes and the tube was making an occasional ping as the messages flew past. And then the conveyor suddenly disappeared upwards vertically and we went on around the curve of a little obsolete tramway and light came through thick glass bricks let into the roof. Alec told us we had passed under Broad Street and the old Bodleian buildings and quadrangle and were beneath the lawns of Radcliffe Square. Then at last we came through swing doors into another underground bookstore with an astonishing iron-grilled floor which had yet another bookstore underneath with a tiny iron staircase and we could see a man working at a desk below the grill. Mr Elliot said he looked to have been down there forever.

'Then we climbed the staircase into the lower Camera which looks so cosy with its soft-shaded reading-lamps under the arched alcoves. We envied you being able to read there. And when we climbed on again up the main spiral staircase and entered the Upper Camera Carlotta and I exclaimed with delight at the great domed ceiling, and Mr Elliot said, 'But how do they manage to heat this place?' A member of staff who was passing hissed that they didn't manage and it was damn cold in winter, and a few readers looked up with disapproving expressions, reminding us to be quiet.

'Well Alec took us down the main staircase again and outside into Radcliffe Square to walk above-ground to the Old Bodley and as we came under the archway into the quadrangle he said he hoped

Bodley's Librarian would see him in such distinguished company. I knew he meant Carlotta because she looked absolutely stunning as usual, – and I must say Walter looked very proud and handsome too on her other side. Mr Elliot and I were lagging slightly behind

'Carlotta said there was a special exhibition of early philosophical works which she would like to see, and Alec told her it was in the Divinity School where we were just going. He said he'd been to the sherry party for the opening but hadn't had time have a good look himself yet.'

'My dear Emmie, it's always the same, and makes the Bodleian staff very frustrated. They take months putting together special collections of unknown incunabula and writing descriptive catalogues, and while scholars from all over the world come especially to see them, people here who should be interested can hardly bother to look.'

'Well Alec did have a good look this time because Carlotta had been reading one of those very catalogues over lunch, – I told you she eats very little, – and of course she wanted Alec to explain more...'

'I begin to understand the fatal charm! But wasn't it rather tedious for you and your Mr Elliot?'

'Oh no Jan, not at all. The Divinity School is so beautiful, – that fan-vaulted roof! And the view upwards through the huge windows, – the glass had a greenish shimmering effect from the trees, and through the trees the Dome of the Camera was all pinky gold in the sunset, – I simply can't describe...'

'You are doing very well, dear. I must take another look myself sometime.'

'So you see Mr Elliot and I were quite content to sit on those raised up pews at the end and just rest and gaze.'

'But what about Walter?'

'He was with the others, – and I never gave a thought to how tired he must be getting, which always makes him cross.'

'Blind, selfish creature! Cocooned in happiness and guilt and unable to see what's going on under your nose!'

'Well I soon woke up when they beckoned, and Alec said that we must go upstairs to Duke Humphry's Library and Walter said huffily 'Surely we haven't got to climb more stairs!' And Alec replied that we'd hardly begun to see the best of Bodley, and at that

Walter said, 'Then why hadn't we begun at the beginning?' Which made Alec suggest that Walter should 'take a pew' until we came down again, – but Walter came up anyway and of course Alec was right about the best being still to come, but I could see that Walter was in one of his moods from being overtired.'

'He didn't behave himself?'

'Well he was quiet enough walking round, but became awfully surly again when Alec invited us to dinner tomorrow evening at College, – which was exactly what Walter had asked me to arrange for Carlotta to begin with! I do hope Alec wasn't offended...'

'My dear no, by that time Alec was as blind as the rest of you. He told me when he came in that at long last he'd met a woman who understands that philosophers are the advanced guard of civilised thought! And of course he also remembered that Horace is dining in London tomorrow so he would have College all to himself, so to speak, and could arrange a dinner-party. Well dear, I told him I would join you to make up the number, – I am determined not to be left out of that gathering!'

'Oh Jan how super! I've been longing to see you!'

'It means missing one of the Seminar evenings but they are well shuffled together now and probably won't notice if I'm there or not...'

'And I do so want you to meet Mr Elliot and Carlotta...'

'My dear Emmie, I simply can't wait!'

'Janice! How lovely to see you!'

'Emmie dear, you look blooming.'

'It is so lovely to be in Oxford again... – and Janice, here is Mrs Elliot.'

'How do you do. I am Carlotta. May I call you Janice?'

'Of course, I think of you as Carlotta already, Emmie has told me so much, – but everyone seems to call me Jan, – except my husband.'

'And this is Mr Elliot, Jan.'

'Mr Elliot, – I am delighted to meet you at last.'

'Everyone seems to call me Mr Elliot, – but I am reconciled.'

'Janice my dear, we must take our guests up to my room for drinks.'

'Shouldn't you show Carlotta the gardens first, Alec, – it will be dark soon.'

'I long to see some of your rare climbers...'

'Of course, – we can go through this little door. Janice, will you follow with the others? I'm afraid the paths are very narrow, Mrs Elliot.'

'Do please call me Carlotta. And may I call you Alec?'

'But of course, – and when we have looked around the garden, Carlotta, I have a special treat for you upstairs...'

'Hadn't you better wear your coat, Carlotta?'

'Walter, – how sweet of you to carry it. Yes, thanks, that is more comfortable.'

'...as I was saying, Carlotta, there is a special item of interest for you upstairs. I have asked the Librarian to let me have the Lacoste Book of Hours in my room to show you, – it is our most treasured possession...'

'My God, Emmie! Did you hear that? Clarence has allowed their precious Book of Hours out of the Library. Horace would have a fit! Mr Elliot, there seems to be room for three on this walk. Could you take my arm?'

'Alec! This wall is a veritable sun-trap, – I have never seen this variety of Bignonia growing so far north before...'

'Your wife is very knowledgeable Mr Elliot.'

'Yes, I must say Lottie knows what she is about when it comes to plants.'

'...this is a magnificent specimen. And its smell, Alec! – a blend of vanilla and pineapple...'

'Delightful! With a hint of almond perhaps? Don't mind my toes, Walter, have a good long sniff while you are about it. There are some beautiful climbers along here, Carlotta. Let me give you a hand, – the path is slippery...'

'I'm afraid, Mr Elliot, that my husband doesn't know a geranium from a petunia. But I suggest that we wait on this bench in the sun. Yes, that's a relief, I've been on my legs all day. I was about to remark that the Master should have been here to show Carlotta around, – he is said to know the name of every plant, – which is perhaps the nicest side of his character. But my God, Emmie! Do you see what I see? There is Horace, – the man himself! Coming this way! And Alec must have seen him too, he has turned down another path! But he will never escape Horace on his own ground. We can hardly avoid introductions. This is going to be interesting!'

'My dear Janice! We are honoured, – you have been neglecting us of late. We don't see you here often enough.'

'And it seems I nearly missed you this time, Horace. They told us you were dining in London.'

'I like the metropolis less and less, and decided to come home before dark…'

'May I introduce… but no doubt you remember my friend, Emma?'

'Of course. How could a Janite ever forget?'

'And this is Mr Elliot, – Sir Horace…'

'How do you do. A lovely evening for your visit. But didn't I see Alec disappearing with the rest of your party, Janice?'

'Yes, he is attempting to show Mrs Elliot and Walter your garden. Mrs Elliot is a great plantswoman.'

'Indeed? Then may I ask you to introduce me? They went to the left…'

'It looks to me, Emmie, that Sir Horace likes to keep his finger on the pulse!'

'Oh dear, Alec will be so put out, – they don't get on at all well. And supposing Sir Horace finds out about the Book of Hours?'

'Perhaps Janice will find a way to disengage them, – though goodness knows how long that may take if Sir Horace is as keen on rare plants as Lottie is. I am beginning to feel the pangs. It must be nearly dinnertime, and my digestive juices started working as soon as I read in 'The Academic Gourmet' that this college serves the best food in Oxford. Are you hungry Emmie?'

'Starving!'

'Well let's hope the publicity hasn't lost the College its cook.'

'Look! Janice is coming back, – but only with Alec, – and Walter is following…'

'For God's sake, woman! Whatever made you let Horace in on our party?'

'Please don't swear, Alec. Horace insisted and introductions were inevitable. Walter dear, the path is so slippery, – would you take my arm? I am so happy to have you and Emmie here again. We can enjoy a chat at least while we are waiting. Please don't get up, Mr Elliot, let me sit on this side...Will you sit down Walter?'

'No thank you, Janice, I will keep on the move with Alec.'

'My God, Emmie, what are we going to do about Horace and the Book? Have you a solution Mr Elliot?'

'You mean that I might call off my wife? That is easier said than done, I'm afraid. But why don't you and Alec take Emmie up to his room now the sun is going? Walter and I will wait here for Lottie, and then there will be no need to invite Sir Horace.'

'Ah you don't know the Master, Mr Elliot. Horace will muscle in on the party somehow if he wants to, – he would insist on escorting you upstairs, – and then...'

'Well perhaps we could go straight in to dinner and not return to your husband's room until afterwards...'

'How clever, there is our hope. Are you warm enough Emmie?'

'But look Jan! They are coming back already!'

'Oh God, so they are, we must think up another escape. Not a word about the Book!'

'My apologies, dear people, I had quite lost track of time until Mrs Elliot reminded me...'

'Yes it will soon be too dark to appreciate Sir Horace's treasury of plants and he has kindly invited me to come again tomorrow for a longer look...'

'So now I suggest we all step into my lodging for a drink before I have the honour of taking you into Hall for dinner. I see they have put on an excellent menu in spite of my absence. Mrs Elliot, I think you will find my modest quarters are not without interest.'

'Sir Horace, you are joking! I know you are housed in one of Oxford's architectural gems. I understand it is the oldest Master's Lodging still in use...'

'Yes, fortunately we escaped the rebuilding of the nineteenth century, – our foundation was poorly endowed, and we reap the benefit now.'

'It is an exquisite building outside, Sir Horace, – but perhaps I could have a peep at the interior tomorrow. You see Alec has a treat for us too. He has promised to show us your fabulous possession, – the Lacoste Book of Hours.'

'Then it is most opportune that I returned early. Our Librarian is dining out and I have the only other key. We will go to the Library at once if you wish...'

'The Book is in my room, Master.'

'That is impossible! Clarence has strict instructions...'

'Alec persuaded Clarence, Horace. As you know Alec was also custodian for many years. Mrs Elliot was anxious to see the Book, – and we have only now heard that she intends to stay over tomorrow...'

'In that case, Alec, perhaps you would be good enough to bring the Book over to my lodging for Mrs Elliot to see. Then I can lock it up again overnight.'

'Oh Alec! Would you be an angel and do that? It would be delightful to see the Master's Lodging and the Book together!'

'Here then, Mrs Elliot, we come upon the little door leading into the humble abode of Masters over the centuries.'

'Be it ever so humble, Sir Horace, it is an honour to enter!'

'But be careful of the steps down inside, – the passage is very narrow I'm afraid, – let me give you a hand. Will the others please follow our lead?'

'He doesn't mean you, 'Angel'. You've got to hurry along and do the Master's bidding!'

'Don't hiss, Janice. I can't hear a word you are saying.'

'None so deaf! Don't get left behind, Walter.'

'I think I might accompany Alec, – unless you have any objection, Alec?'

'My dear fellow, of course not...'

'Then shall Emmie and I go first, Mr Elliot? We can tumble down these steps hand in hand. My dear Emmie, your Carlotta is fabulous!'

'I knew you would like her...'

'And it seems that in spite of your fears Walter and Alec are still good friends. Look out for that beam, Mr Elliot, – oh dear, too late!'

'God help me, Walter, – there are times when I could hit that man!'

'I never encountered a more obnoxious oaf in all my days!'

'...and just now I was ready to strike him dead!'

'My dear Alec, I am not surprised, I felt inclined to have a bash at him myself...'

'My God, if we both had fallen upon him! That would have caused a furore! I suggest we have a drink before we go back. What do you say?'

AUNT JESSIE'S BLESSING

'Binns End 201'

'Emma? My dear I was so shattered by the tragic news... I had to telephone at once...But are you not out shopping this morning?'

'No, Walter went today, – he needed a hair-cut...'

'But to read of Sir Horace's death, Emma, – in The Times just now! I felt I simply must talk to... – to a mutual friend. Poor Sir Horace, such a kindly man! Did you know he was ill?'

'No Carlotta, we hardly knew him, – but it was a shock for everyone, especially poor Alec. Janice rang me last evening. Apparently he and Sir Horace were together in the College garden when the Master fell dead at Alec's feet...'

'Emma, how terrible! One can imagine his distress, – I'm sure they were very close. When I read that Sir Horace died in his famous garden it brought back to me that last lovely evening in Oxford, and do you know I had the strangest fancy that perhaps Sir Horace was remembering me too, – he sent me the sweetest letter not too long ago. But I can see now I was being foolishly sentimental. If Alec was with him they were no doubt discussing weighty matters. Sir Horace hinted even to me that the problems of College administration hung heavily on his shoulders. These high-powered men, Emma, they just work themselves into the ground...'

'Oh I hardly think so, Carlotta, Janice always says...'

'And I assure you Sidney was just as bad. How thankful he is that I persuaded him to retire. He swears it saved his life.'

'Is he keeping well?'

'Yes indeed, – in fact, Emma, we were just talking of our spring visit to Cornwall, and I was brimming with ideas, – but now I feel...well I don't feel like planning anything.'

'Do you have to go?'

'Oh yes, indeed we must. Nan writes that poor darling Mummy is getting very frail. I must simply gather myself together and not be selfish. Sidney said this morning that in the midst of death we are still in life so we might as well get on with it, – which sounded very unfeeling in the circumstances, – but is true I suppose. We were hoping, Emma, – as we missed the Spas this year, – that you and Walter might join us on a leisurely tour to Cornwall, – in the Delage…'

'Oh Carlotta, that would be super, but I'm afraid Walter will never take the Delage on a long journey again, or drive her fast on motorways…'

'I do understand his concern. But perhaps he can be persuaded, – do you mind if I ring him again?'

'Of course not, please do.'

'Within a few days then, I shall have some details to work out. And Emma, please do send Alec my sympathy in the meanwhile.'

'So, Emmie, what do you think about this trip to Cornwall the Elliots are proposing? In the Delage?'

'My dear Walter, I've already told Carlotta that you wouldn't risk the Delage on the motorways.'

'But Carlotta has worked out a special itinerary to avoid them, using the old country lanes in fact. She proposes to take several days and stop at interesting places on the way.'

'It sounds most tempting dear. But I would advise you to play safe and go in the Metro.'

'Oh don't be so absurd, Emmie. Carlotta hasn't planned an itinerary like that for the Metro. As she points out the whole charm of the journey will be in using country roads which existed when the Delage was new, and staying in old country inns and not having to hurry ourselves.'

'Oxford 98245'

'Janice, I've got the most exciting news. We are going to Cornwall with the Elliots!'

'Congratulations Emmie. How did you manage it?'

'It was Carlotta's idea. She has persuaded Walter to take the Delage again. To cheer her up, she says. I told you she was terribly upset last week about poor Sir Horace.'

'My God, Emmie, do you know Alec can't get over it either. I've never seen him so knocked up. He hasn't even glanced at his own work since it happened.'

'Alec? Well perhaps he was quite fond of Sir Horace underneath.'

'My dear Emmie, I fear it is guilt rather than fondness. You see Alec so often said that he felt ready to strike Horace dead, and my guess is that when they were in the garden together Horace did say something intensely annoying which made Alec ready to strike him down. And in the next moment there was Horace lying at his feet...'

'It must have been a terrible shock.'

'Yes, the physical shock put him in a state of jitters, – and his situation is so unnerving. Alec has so much to gain from Horace's death.'

'Alec will be Master now?'

'I don't think they can pass him over this time, – and I dare say he will do a good job once he pulls himself together. I only wish I wasn't going away at this time, – but the trip is finally organised...'

'How long will you be in America?'

'Longer than I expected, – there is the spell at Berkeley, as you know, – and an unexpected bonus, Emmie. My book is selling well in the States...'

'Your 'Matrons and Matriarchs of the late Eighteenth Century'?'

'It seems that Americans like long titles.'

'Well I loved it. Is there any more news of your main work getting printed?'

'Hopeless Emmie, still languishing in the hands of The Press, while this frivolous offshoot, published in the States, is going down so well with American matrons that my agent has booked a lecture-tour of women's clubs, – coast to coast.'

'Goodness, how terrifying!'

'I think I might enjoy it. They specially like my chapter about Princess Lubomirska and Ben Franklin.'

'Well Jan, rather you than me. You certainly deserve success.'

'Don't I just, – somewhat ill-timed, I fear, but too late to cancel now. When do you start your holiday, Emmie?'

'Next week, – the Elliots are joining us here for a night before we set out. I've got just six days to get ready.'

'Some more coffee Carlotta?'

'Yes please, Walter. May we help with the washing-up Emma?'

'It's all done, thank you Carlotta. I stacked the machine while the coffee was brewing.'

'My dear how well-organised you are, – and such a delicious meal. Do you think we might indulge ourselves with a glance at the maps now? I have plotted a charming route, I think, hardly touching any main roads, – but not suitable for road-hogs, Walter, so no speeding, I'm afraid. We must content ourselves with wandering along the byways, – soaking up the history of England as we go. Did you bring the map-case from the car, Sidney?'

'I could hardly stagger in with it, – you must have packed the entire Ordnance Survey.'

Country lanes are not marked on ordinary maps. Ah, thank you Walter. May we spread out here? I have them all in succession, – but perhaps you had better sit by me, Emma...'

'Oh no, I'm sure Walter will understand the route better than I can...'

'But my dear, – if Walter is driving you will have to map-read...'

'Carlotta, I couldn't possibly, – I am so dim with maps...'

'Ah – then Sydney and I will have to blaze the trail in the Rover with you and Walter following...'

'But that is not quite what you intend, Lottie, is it? So let's agree without more ado that since you have plotted the trail you must blaze it with Walter in the Delage, – and since Emmie and I are both duffers at map-reading we will have to follow in the Rover as your back-up team.'

'You are right, Sidney, that will probably be best, – if you're sure you don't mind, Emma.'

'Oxford 98245'

'Our last chat, Jan, before I get to bed. Can't afford telephone calls to California.'

'I shall depend on you to write to me, Em. No one else will.'

'And I suppose I shall only get cards back.'

'That's right. I promise to send one every time I get a nice long letter. So you are off on your tour to Cornwall? But I don't see how it can take you more than a day to get there.'

'We plan to wander along the byways, stopping here and there and soaking up the history of England as we go.'

'No need to ask the source of that quote!'

'Well Carlotta has a point. We do neglect our own countryside. I've never visited Wells or Glastonbury. And it will be lovely not to hurry. How is Alec? I can imagine how worried you must be about leaving him.'

'Not so much now, – I think he will adjust to the upheaval, he has so many pressing concerns and of course he can live at ease in College. It seems that everyone feels the easing of tension. That perhaps is the real tragedy, that poor Horace has nobody to mourn him. He exasperated most people one way or another in the end.'

'Has Alec taken to his own work again?'

'I'm afraid that has been put aside for the while, indefinitely, I shouldn't wonder. If Alec does become Master he will be first and foremost a fund-raiser to pay for restoring the fabric of the buildings, – and he will be on a number of committees, – ex-officio. Horace was very useful in that respect, and as you know he never forgot a name. Alec even has difficulty remembering faces, – but they are already feeling him out to chair the national 'Battels' committee.'

'So he is likely to become Sir Alec someday?'

'That may be his fate in the end I fear.'

'Comfortable Emmie?'

'Blissful thanks.'

'And warm enough?'

'Super, – and thankful I'm not travelling in the open car.'

'This arrangement seems to suit everyone. Look how cheery our opposite pair are, bouncing along in Uncle Albert's Memorial.'

'Oh please don't remind me. I have to keep my fingers crossed as it is.'

'A touch of Aunt Jessie shivers?'

'If only one could be sure she doesn't mind.'

'Well I expect she does disapprove sometimes. I see ghosts as quirky characters and one can imagine them getting exasperated by what goes on here below. But sometimes perhaps she is gratified, – Aunt Jessie was probably quite proud of Walter's success at Blenheim...'

'I can't forget that feeling of baleful influence when we were driving in that awful weather on the Milan autostrada, – and then the breakdown!'

'I expect your nerves were overtaxed that day...oh damn... that tractor is turning out behind the Delage, – we shall never overtake the fellow in these lanes. Let's hope we don't lose the trail-blazers.'

'I expect they will wait at the next crossroad, – Carlotta will be sure to notice. Tell me, is she like her mother?'

'Physically there is a strong resemblance, – but no, I don't think Sophie ever had Lottie's capacity, – and I'm afraid her wits have deteriorated with her health in recent years. I am wondering what we shall find this time.'

'Carlotta mentions a person called Nan who is devoted to her mother. Was she Carlotta's nanny?'

'Nan? No, her name is Ann as a matter of fact, – she is a sort of cousin, a retired nurse, and she is devoted, thank God. We are very lucky. Oh good, the tractor is turning right...'

'But no sign of the Delage.'

'Botheration – and it's a T-junction, with no sign-post either, – which way do you suppose they went?'

'Possibly the tractor went down a lane to a farm, it looks awfully muddy...'

'Good thinking, Emmie, we will try turning left. Thank goodness we know the name of the village, and the inn where we are to lie tonight, as Lottie puts it.'

> Dear Janice,
>
> We have reached Devonshire and I have a chance to write while the others are watching a T.V. film which I've seen twice already which Carlotta missed while abroad. In fact I would not have expected television to be her thing but she has been an avid watcher these last evenings in hotels. On our first night we were none of us fit for anything except flopping out in front of the screen. I was worn out from organising our getaway, and Carlotta had come in somewhat shattered after getting lost with Walter in the Delage. Not surprising since she has planned our route through a maze of lanes to avoid main roads, – an enchanting drive in unspoiled country which I have enjoyed immensely.

Mr Elliot and I were in the Rover following the 'trail-blazers' but when the cars got separated by a tractor we got lost too, having no maps, and we drove a long way not knowing where we were. Mr Elliot said Lottie should have left bunches of twigs at the crossroads, but then, unexpectedly, we came to the inn where we were to 'lie that night' (quote, unquote) and Mr Elliot was very proud of himself for having made landfall, as he put it, by dead reckoning.

But there was no sign of the Delage and we were very concerned, – it was no good going back to search for them in such a maze of lanes. Mr Elliot said no more driving around in circles for him, we must go inside and wait in comfort for a telephone call.

After a while the Delage did drive in under its own power but plastered in mud. It appeared that they had turned right instead of left where we lost them and the tractor turned in behind them and they had to drive along the lane for a mile before they could turn round in a muddy farmyard and then the tractor swept in and splashed the car with cow-dung. And then they went wrong again coming out and realised they were driving back the way we had come. No wonder poor Carlotta was fagged out, – it is very tiring just travelling in the Delage, as I well know.

Luckily her clothes didn't get muddy because she was wearing, if you will believe it, a boiler-suit made of white leather! And as she says leather feels the cold on account of being shorn she wears over it a finger-length coat of fox fur. Her husband warns her of the danger of wearing real fox these days in country lanes. And he warns Walter to look out for packs of animal-rights fanatics who might tear our navigator to pieces, – because nobody else can read the maps.

So you see we are all very cheerful together and on these last days the laps have been shorter. We stayed another night at Bradford-on-Avon, a charming town which I had never even heard of before, and we have visited Wells and Glastonbury, – but please don't groan, – I will restrain myself from writing a travelogue. Tomorrow we drive deep into Devonshire and are to 'lie' at a Manor hotel. The next day we should reach our journey's end at Trevelgue Manor on the north Cornish coast where we are invited to stay for a few weeks. And there lives Carlotta's 'darling mummy' whose wits, I am told, are somewhat astray, – with her nurse-companion (or perhaps guardian?) who is called Nan. Oh dear, I don't know why, but writing this down has given me a little shiver of fear. I wonder what awaits us?

'Emma! I see you are revelling in the luxuriance of this garden.'

'It is delightful. The whole valley is beautiful...'

'This is our last chance to indulge ourselves among gentle hills and lush vegetation.'

'....and each place you have chosen to stay in, Carlotta, has been such a contrast to the one before.'

'Ah, tomorrow you will see contrast indeed in the austere grandeur of Trevelgue, – the magnificent cliffs of my dear wild Trevelgue...background to the story of Tristan and Isolde, – we will listen to Wagner in the moonlight...'

'I hope you've both got a good head for heights. Lottie's enthusiasm for precipitous cliffs gives me vertigo just at the thought.'

'Don't exaggerate, Sidney. But how glad I am that we are here in time for the primroses. I cannot bear to think of a year going by without seeing primroses in their natural setting...'

'These pale wild flowers are exquisite.'

'Yes Emma, I find the charm of this garden is its natural state, and yet it is filled with sub-tropical plants. Some of the exotics take me back to that wonderful evening in Oxford. Doesn't it remind you of Alec's College, Walter? And poor dear Sir Horace?'

'I don't think, Lottie, that Walter remembers Sir Horace as being especially poor or dear.'

'There is no need to be uncharitable, Sidney. What news do you have of Alec, Emma?'

'Only what Janice told me before she left, – it seems he has little time for academic work now. In addition to his other chores, as Janice calls them, he has been invited to chair the Battels Committee...

'Battels, – how quaint! Do they still have them? Coals and candles and food, are they not?'

'Well Battels is how they refer to the committee in Oxford, but I understand it is a nation-wide survey of student grants and living conditions.'

'How prestigious! So it will be known by Alec's name in the end, I expect. But, alas, he will never have time for any more guided tours, – his kindness in showing us Bodley gave me such ambition to delve further, Emma. Don't you agree that we really should visit Oxford again – all together. In the autumn perhaps. What does everyone think?'

Trevelgue Manor

Dear Janice,

We set off out of Devonshire this morning under a sky which threatened rain, – so up went the hood of the Delage and a jumble of prayers from me. Firstly that the rain would keep off, secondly to placate Aunt Jessie if it didn't, and thirdly of plain thankfulness that I was travelling in the Rover.

Walter had been jittery early on, up and outside before anyone else, fidgeting with the side-screens. But then Carlotta came down to breakfast and our spirits lightened in spite of the heavy sky. She too had observed the weather and was dressed in an ordinary denim suit, transformed by her effortless casual elegance. I don't know how she does it, but she cheers us all up with her unfailing good-humour and optimism. Her husband is obviously proud of her and Walter admiring, though he affects not to notice her clothes. And I am always more at ease when the men are happy, not to mention that we had such a super breakfast, starting with porridge which I really shouldn't touch, but can't resist, topped with brown sugar and cream. Mr Elliot says I am rounding out nicely so I fear it shows, – and I promised myself that after eating such a huge breakfast I would forego lunch, which of course I didn't.

The extraordinary thing is that when I am slimming at home and give breakfast a miss, and then dash about doing things I often don't feel like lunch, whereas on the road, after doing nothing all morning, a three-course breakfast seems to have given me a raging appetite by noon and I look forward eagerly to our midday stop. Today we had planned to have our main meal early to save Nan in the evening. And a very poor meal it turned out to be, very slow, with a bleak tedious drive afterwards which took much longer than expected.

Fortunately the rain kept off, with an occasional flurry out of lowering clouds, but it was quite dark when we reached here. We left behind the lights of the hamlet and the last houses, turning off the road into darkness and nothing could be seen on either side of a rough driveway, quite a mile long, I should say, which leads to the house. Only far away in the distance there was a flickering light, appearing and disappearing as the drive dipped and curved, – a light which was somehow sinister rather than welcoming, – and that was Trevelgue Manor, Mr Elliot told me.

He had warned us that the manor house was very isolated, having been protected by the National Trust for many years from neighbouring development. While we were still in the middle of England this warning had sounded romantic and interesting. But approaching it on a dark blustery night I began to feel that the proper place for a manor house should be in a cosy valley, protecting its own village, and not stuck away on a remote windswept cliff. And that this was certainly not a suitable habitation for a frail old woman and her nurse-companion. Or even for a wild mad woman and her guardian! Was that perhaps the explanation?

Remembering Mr Elliot's doubt when he was wondering what they might find this time, I was suddenly struck by how little we knew of any of them, – how slight was our acquaintance. The Delage, lurching and bumping along the road ahead was in itself an anachronism which had plucked Walter and I out of our everyday lives. Into what was it leading us now?

The flickering light which had been growing brighter suddenly disappeared, and so did the Delage, swallowed into a windswept hedgerow, and we followed through a gap, an open gateway almost completely arched over by bent thorn. We arrived in a kind of courtyard and before us loomed a gaunt house with a light over its doorway. At that moment the door was thrown open by a pleasant-looking woman, and Carlotta jumped down from the Delage and ran to kiss her. This was Nan, – kindly, sensible, welcoming, and far from being the Grace Poole of my foolish imagination.

Nan led us into a large comfortable room with a bright fire, beside which sat a ninety-year old replica of Carlotta. The resemblance was uncanny. Sophie, as we have been told to call her, greeted us quite lucidly, apologising for not getting up and hoping we were not too fatigued by the journey. To my surprise Carlotta did not rush to kiss her mother as she had done to Nan. Then after a pause she came from behind, and Sophie cried, 'Charlotte, my Charlotte!' And Carlotta went and knelt beside her, clasping her mother's frail body in her arms, and they both wept.

Nan whispered to me that she would take us up to our room and as we went upstairs she told us that she must first put Sophie to bed and then we could eat, – just some soup and cold meat, she explained. She showed us into a large room, rather austere but nice and warm from central heating, and left us to wash our hands.

Walter peered through the curtains but all he could see was rain, coming down heavily at last, beating against the pane, and I knew he was anxious to get the car under cover so I hurried up to come down with him. I felt tired and wished very much that we were staying in an hotel, anonymous, independent, not bothering other people and not involved with their emotions.

Carlotta was still kneeling by her mother who seemed to have fallen asleep, – she got up quietly and whispered to Walter that Sidney was unloading the cars and would show him where to put the Delage. They crept from the room, shutting the door quietly, but the click of the lock brought the old lady bolt awake again. She seemed quite pleased to see me so I sat down on the other side of the fire feeling a little more at ease, until she quite unnerved me my asking if I had heard that her daughter Charlotte was coming tomorrow. Well of course, if I'd had a grain of sense I would have gone along with her delusion, instead of which I stupidly tried to explain that Charlotte had already arrived, and had only just gone out of the room.

A weird wild gleam came into the old woman's eye. 'No, no,' she said, 'They are misleading you again. That was my sister, Athelie! And when Charlotte comes you will see that she is not like Athelie at all.' It was not so much her words, Jan, as the look she fixed on me, – for the first time ever in my life I felt my hairs wanting to stand up, – a distinct prickly feeling around the back of my neck. Then the old woman became querulous. 'Where is Nan?' she demanded. 'Where are my spectacles? I have Charlotte's letter by me somewhere, I will show you.'

I noticed that her glasses were beside her on a small table, lying on a letter from Carlotta which had obviously been read many times, and I passed them to her.

'I knew she would come,' she said, smoothing the letter without attempting to read it. 'Charlotte loves this place, you know. We used to come here every summer when she was a child. That is why I chose this house to settle in, although Athelie said I was crazy! It would never bring Charlotte back, she said. But I know Charlotte will come.'

Suddenly Sophie leaned forward and grasped my hand. 'Don't trust Athelie,' she hissed. 'One shouldn't speak ill of one's sister, – but I can tell you, Athelie is a mean spiteful creature!' And really, Jan, the venomous expression in the old woman's eye, distorted and magnified by her spectacles, made me cold with fright.

Luckily at that moment Nan breezed back into the room with a gust of sanity, telling Sophie it was time for 'beddy-byes' and using other comfortable expressions which were soothing to both of us. Sophie was content to be led upstairs, and I was only too happy to bustle round and help carry her bits and pieces. Nan seemed glad of my company because she kept talking of this and that, so I stayed until Sophie was tucked into bed. There seemed to be no expectation that Carlotta would come to wish her mother goodnight, which surprised me. I couldn't remark on it of course.

But as we were going downstairs a question of great moment did pop out of me. I was dying to know if Athelie was still alive. 'Very much so!' Nan replied to my great relief. It had occurred to me that perhaps she might be dead and I felt that a second ghost besides Aunt Jessie would be simply too much to cope with. 'So you have heard about Athelie?' Nan asked, and I told her what had happened.

She said that Sophie and Athelie had always struck sparks off each other, – Athelie was rather bossy but she never ventured to Trevelgue since Sophie became a little peculiar, – which was only from age, Nan explained, as if anxious to maintain the honour of the family.

Well, we have all retired early after eating supper, – too soon perhaps because my mind can't settle to let me sleep, but Walter has gone out like a light, – so I can have mine on to write this. Carlotta still seemed near to tears this evening and Walter was very attentive, – which made me impatient. It begins to look as if she is entirely selfish, – her mother living in such a remote place to tempt her back and Carlotta visiting only for a few weeks, and at that it would seem rather to enjoy the primroses. And not even bothering to climb the stairs to wish her mother goodnight, – well!

Jan, I was woken by a shaft of sunlight through the curtain, – the weather has cleared and I discovered that the curtains draw straight across a deep bay-window so I have been able to creep through them to sit on a window-seat and continue this without disturbing Walter.

Looking out over the sea gives one the impression of being in the poop of a ship, the house is so near the edge of the cliff with a precipitous drop below. By pressing my nose to the glass I can see that there is a strip of garden under the house bounded by a low hedge with a wicket gate to the cliff path. But the view this morning, Jan! And the colours – I really can't describe, – I can just hear you saying I am going to try to anyway, – so I will. The cliffs are as magnificent as Carlotta has claimed, they curve round the bay ending in rocky headlands, just ready to be painted, but there is no sign of a harbour. Not even a beach can be seen from the window, only an expanse of deep blue sea with a great slow swell breaking white against the rocks.

I am wondering what the day will bring. The thing is that in spite of everything I like Carlotta, and I'm not at all sure that I am going to like Sophie. But what I am dying for now is a cup of tea so I think I will creep downstairs to see if anyone else is up.

'Can I do anything to help, Nan?'

'Good heavens, my dear! You gave me quite a start! Are you usually such an early riser? Did you have a comfortable night?'

'Lovely, thanks, – but it is such a lovely morning I couldn't stay in bed...'

'The tea is only just brewed if you'd care to join me.'

'I'd love a cup, Nan.'

'I always sit for a while to enjoy mine. This is the quietest moment of the day...Milk?'

'Yes please, I do hope I'm not disturbing you...'

'My dear, not at all, it is nice to have someone to talk to, but once Sophie is awake –and the women come, well you can imagine...'

'You manage to get help then? The house is so isolated.'

'Yes, the domestic situation is much easier since our helpers took to driving, – and owning their own cars. All that bothers us now is mechanical breakdown, but with two we manage pretty well.'

'You are lucky. It is impossible to persuade anyone from our village to come to us, though we don't live as far from the village as this...'

'Ah, there is Sophie's bell. Everybody wakeful this morning! I had better take up breakies.'

'Can I help?'

'No dear, I have it all ready for her on a tray, – exactly the same thing every day or she gets upset. Why don't you have a look around the garden until Charlotte comes down to tell us what to do with the day?'

> Jan –
>
> They tell me that the post-office van collects letters in the mornings, so just a few more words before I seal up. We had a lovely walk this morning to the headland from which the ruins of Tintagel castle can be seen far away in the distance. Carlotta told us the story of Tristan and Isolde, bringing it to life quite magically, – she says it is based on historical fact, – and this evening we are to listen to Wagner. Just a potted version, Mr Elliot assured us, – on a cassette, Carlotta added, which captures the essence.
>
> We came back to lunch blown full of fresh air, and then went for a short drive this afternoon, – taking Sophie to give Nan a break. She was quite lucid today and you should have seen

how happy she was to be out with Carlotta, – who is just now putting her to bed. So it really looks that the poor old thing would be quite compos mentis if only Carlotta could be with her more. Of course Carlotta has to consider her husband – but then he seems to go along with whatever she plans. I do feel though that he is happy we are here, and so I think is Nan who is going to visit friends this evening, she confided to me that she is not very musical and wants to escape a feast of Wagner.

'Rapturous! Emma, didn't you feel yourself transported into another world?'

'Well…yes, I was dreaming…'

'One cannot fail to recognise the magnificent sweep of our cliffs in the music. How did it affect you, Walter?'

'It certainly makes a difference where one listens. I've never before…'

'What we must do now is just sit perfectly quiet, – listening to the sea. Do you mind if I throw up a window? I love these great sash windows…'

'Steady on there, Lottie, the mouse…'

'…oh dear, it has jammed…'

'I was just warning you, Lottie. Nan tells me the mouse has fallen in…'

'Mouse?'

'Let me help, Carlotta, it is dangerous to leave it half-way. The mouse is a counter-weight which helps lift the window smoothly. I will give you a hand in the morning, Elliot, – to take it down…'

'My dear Walter, I never tangle with jobs like that!'

'It is quite straightforward, – you only have to unscrew the beading here. Just look…'

'Yes, I see what you mean, – we'll have a look tomorrow, perhaps…'

'Really Emma! Trust those men to destroy our rapture… let me sit by you…'

'Shall I prop the window open, Carlotta?'

'Thank you Walter, that is better, now at last we can sit quietly. And how quiet the sea is tonight. Can you not imagine Tristan navigating his little barque?'

'I wonder how they did navigate, with no chronometer?'

'Lunar, I expect, Walter.'

'But it is so often cloudy...'

'Yes indeed, – but obviously he didn't pile her up in this bay. I wonder if Isolde got seasick?'

'Stop it, Sidney! Walter you are just as bad! Emma, you are the only silent one. Tell me, don't you sometimes feel your soul wanting to take wings, – back into a simpler world, – away from this dreadful consumer society?'

'Well I do rather appreciate...'

'I feel it so strongly when I am walking on the cliffs. My spirit longs to rise and float on the wind with the sea-birds. I have always said, Emma, that when I die I would wish my ashes to be scattered from these cliffs. Do you hear me, Sidney?'

'I can't help hearing you, my darling, – I'd have to wait for an offshore wind of course. But then with the normal expectation of life I shall be dead long before you are and I assure you that putting me down in our cosy old graveyard alongside my parents will suit me very well. So please don't have any romantic notion of shaking my ashes over these frightening cliffs...it gives me vertigo just at the thought!'

'You are a prosaic old stick-in-the-mud, Sidney!'

'So entirely proper, dear, to dig me into the ground when I conk out...'

'Stop it Sidney, stop! You know how sensitive I am... that I simply can't think of anyone...I have been so happy this evening because Mummy is so much better...and the thought of her frail little body being put under the earth...No, no! You know I cannot bear it...I cannot...'

'Quiet, darling, quiet. I'm sorry Lottie. Come now, – there is Nan driving in. Let us go out to welcome her home.'

Trevelgue Manor

Dear Janice,

Some of the happenings in this house make me wish we were not here, – and at the same time thankful that we are. During the two weeks since I last wrote our visit has been following the usual course –as holiday, – sightseeing in changeable Cornish weather.

We have had some warm sunny days and days of mist or gentle rain – still mild and pleasant to walk in; and in between days of clearing skies and invigorating air with sunshine and colour returning, – marvellous on the cliff tops. The sea is such a deep blue on this north-facing coast, – one misses the glitter, – but the colours! A depth and clarity of blue into green more vivid than the Mediterranean.

As to happenings I hardly know where to start, – from the beginning I was gradually becoming more sorry for Sophie and less patient with Carlotta, whose affection for her mother seemed to be mainly words. And Sophie was so pathetically content in Carlotta's company, behaving quite sensibly like a good child, and I have to say for Carlotta that she became more relaxed and happy in her mother's company too.

Sophie has two themes the moment Carlotta goes out of sight. When she is cheerful she tells me for the umpteenth time that Charlotte is coming tomorrow, picking up the letter which has now become so thin you can almost see through it, always demanding her glasses but never attempting to read. But when she is low in spirits she complains that Charlotte never comes, even if Carlotta has only just left the room, and she will tell me again how she left her real home, as she calls it, because Charlotte loved Trevelgue. But Charlotte never comes, she says, sounding heartbroken, which quite upsets me, she looks so frail and pathetic. And if I happen to touch her, to help her get up, her fragile bones, so lightly covered, strike me with a shock of pity, and I can easily understand Carlotta's horror at the thought of such a frail little body being buried in the ground.

You may be sure that after that first weird encounter I have been careful to go along with Sophie's delusions, – and the dreaded name of Athelie was never mentioned again, – until one terrible day about a week ago. Carlotta was with her mother and both seemed happy, – and then suddenly, for no reason I can remember, though I have tried, Sophie mistook Carlotta for Athelie! I had a fleeting impression that she was pretending, but I must have been mistaken because there was a most terrible scene, – Carlotta trying to reassure her mother, trying to explain, – and Sophie beyond reason, attacking Carlotta with that evil venomous expression which had so unnerved me. Carlotta was terrified, almost in hysterics, and I don't wonder, – I rushed out to fetch Nan who was trying to do some gardening and luckily the men were with her. We all hurried back together into the middle of the row. Nan took Sophie upstairs and Mr Elliot took Carlotta in his arms. I was terribly shaken too and Walter put an arm around me. We were painfully aware of being outsiders, – and yet already emotionally involved. Walter said, 'Carlotta hinted something of this and now one sees what she meant.'

Well, for some days Sophie was quiet and then suddenly, out of the blue, the same thing happened all over again. Poor Carlotta! At last I understand her fear of her mother, – and I must say I prefer to give Sophie a wide berth myself. Even when she is in a good mood she gives me the creeps, so you can imagine why I sometimes wish myself anywhere but here. And yet Carlotta and Mr Elliot and Nan seem so pleased to have our company, as if they rely on us in a way, – and that makes me glad we came.

Now we are off for a walk on the cliffs, in buoyant blustery weather, but we shall feel marvellous when we return, and I shall have the additional satisfaction of having written to you at last.

'Yes, it is young Charlotte I am sorry for...Would you like some more tea, dear? I need at least three cups to get me going in the morning.'

'I'd love another cup, Nan.'

'Poor Charlotte, – it seems that Sophie has an irresistible urge to punish her...'

Nan! You don't mean...? I almost thought so too...but do you mean...really...that Sophie is pretending?'

'I'm not sure, – the pretence is subconscious no doubt, though Sophie always did have a wicked streak and that, I think, is what it stems from. And then, as you've probably heard, Charlotte was a late child...and poor Sophie never got over the loss of her son in the war...'

'Yes, I suppose it is not surprising that she could not bear to lose her daughter. Do you think Carlotta should have stayed?'

'No indeed, Charlotte was too long at home as it was. Of course people say that she is selfish, and I say bully for her that she is. Because Sophie was never content with Charlotte's physical presence, you know, she wanted to control her, body and soul. I am very glad Charlotte escaped, and besides, Sidney is such a dear, – I don't know what we should do without him, – and I'm glad he can afford to let her dress as she does, and to travel, which she always wanted. And then, my dear, if Charlotte had stayed to look after her mother I wouldn't have been needed in my old age and had this comfortable home for retirement, – would I now?'

'You are simply a saint, Nan.'

'Hardly a saint, dear, – a professional, – which is quite different!'

'Sophie is very late with her bell this morning.'

'She was still sleeping peacefully when I looked in, – but one never knows at her age. I had better go and investigate.'

Trevelgue Manor

Dear Janice,

Another week has slipped past, – not altogether peacefully. Sophie keeps us all in a state of jitters, – she seems to have a sixth sense for choosing just the moment when her aberration will cause the most distress. In fact I begin to think she is much better without Carlotta here at all, because when she is expecting her she is quite happy, and Nan says that even when she is complaining about Charlotte never coming this is a good outlet for her ill-humour.

Poor Carlotta is beginning to show the strain, though she is still full of optimism and little plans for the future, – and today, – I am happy to say, – she has 'taken' Walter to a car rally in Truro. Not on such a grand scale as at Blenheim but it will make a nice change. They set off looking so cheerful, and luckily they have a fine day for it. The weather continues very fickle.

Sidney, – there it is written at least, but I am so daft with my shyness about starting to use it that I still avoid calling him anything, and although I have become fond of the name I would really prefer him to remain my dear Mr Elliot. I suppose I am clinging to an outdated world, like Carlotta, only not so far back. I must say her longing to escape into the times of Tristan quite gives me the shudders. Now where was I? Ah yes, well Sidney decided that he and I would do better to stay at home and keep Nan company. It is a good fifty miles to Truro but he says that if the Delage does get into trouble they can always ring up. Preferably a garage, he added, making us laugh as usual. Of course we do feel we are standing by to go to the rescue and get them home if needed.

I am so glad the weather is fine, – dear me I wrote that before, – must avoid repetition. And I do like Nan, – which cannot be repeated often enough. The way she copes with Sophie is really saintly, and although she claims it is just a professional approach I think anyone who goes into the nursing profession must be a saint to start with. My worry now is for Carlotta, – she seems suddenly so vulnerable, not just to her mother's caprice and spite, which is really terrifying, – but even perhaps to her mother's malady. You said Carlotta was brilliant. What do you think? Not that Carlotta ever shows the slightest sign of malice, though she does sometimes snap at her husband, but then he teases her so. Nan says she takes after her father, who must have been a saint too, if you ask me.

I am sitting in the window-seat writing this and am beginning to feel rather cold. This room never gets any sun after morning and now the bay has gone wild and gloomy again, with a great menacing swell crashing against the headland. The wind seems to be getting up, with cloud, but no rain yet thank goodness.

Pressing my nose against the glass I have just noticed that my Mr Elliot is trying to mend the wicket gate to the cliff path, – I thought he was writing letters. He says Walter puts him to shame about doing odd jobs and I suspect he wants to get this fixed before they return, – he will be very proud of himself. I'm glad I haven't been asked to help because I have just done my hair. Walter would have called me down there soon enough to 'Just hold this steady a moment, dear' The hours I've spent crouching in awkward positions and getting cold and blown about! Besides I am keeping an ear for Sophie, she didn't feel like getting up today. I wonder if she knew that Carlotta would not be here? I had better peep in to see if she is O.K.

'Ah –there you are, Sidney. Did you manage to fix the gate?'

'Not very well, I'm afraid, Nan. I've simply botched the job and Walter will jeer when he sees it.'

'Walter is much too polite to jeer.'

'Well smirk then, – we must allow old Walter a smirk. He will politely take it apart and put it back together perfectly, – so I will not begrudge him a smirk. Where is Emmie?'

'Upstairs writing to her friend. She needs some time to herself, you know.'

'I do know, Nan.'

'It is a comfort to have them here. Emmie fits in like family, and Walter cheers up young Charlotte.'

'I know that too, Nan.'

'Dear me, is that the time? We have missed the west-country news...'

'This clock is fast, Nan.'

'Then switch on dear, we might catch the tail-end.'

'Right...Heavens above...that sounds like Lottie! Come on picture! Good grief it is Lottie! With the Delage, and there is Walter! And just look how Lottie is making up to the interviewer...'

'Be quiet, Sidney. I can't hear...'

"...so Mrs Elliot, your magnificent machine has certainly stolen the show. I believe this is the first time we have seen the car in the West Country?"

"Yes indeed, we show very rarely"

'My God, Nan, why haven't we got a video-recorder?'

'Quiet Sidney! Now we have missed what Charlotte was saying, and they have stopped talking. The car looks very well, and look at Walter opening the door for Charlotte...'

'Very gallant! And now back to the studio with the announcer watching the picture too, – on her screen...'

"So there we must leave the Elliots with their magnificent machine..."

'Elliots indeed! She has got it wrong, bless her...'

"...which brings us to the end of the programme. Here again are the headlines..."

'You can switch off now, Sidney. We can't concentrate on news after all that excitement.'

'Well, well. So what do you make of that, Nan?'

'It will appear in the County, Sidney, that you own Walter's motor-car and that he has got your wife. Well we must eat, – you'd better get your hands washed…and call down Emmie as you go.'

> Sophie was dozing, Jan, with Carlotta's letter on the counterpane, it's pathetic really. Well dear, I will address this to Berkeley as you told me, though I expect you are still deep in the Mid-West, lecturing your way across America. As I said, rather you than me! Ah, there is Mr Elliot calling, he must have come in while I wasn't looking. He says we are to have a quiet evening, 'listening for the telephone'!

'They are late, Sidney. Don't you think?'

'Well they would have to stop for a bite to eat, in Truro, or on the road. Please don't start making me nervous, Nan. It looks like being a dirty night and Emmie says that the magnificent machine has a curse on it in bad weather. Have you told Nan, Emmie, about Aunt Jessie and the Albert Memorial? Oh God, – there is the telephone, right on cue…I will go…'

'Whatever nonsense is Sidney blathering now? But he is right about the wind getting up…it's an awful night to be stuck on the road…I don't think you ought to go with him, Emmie…'

'Oh Nan, – I couldn't let him go alone, – for Walter's car!'

'Ah yes, – Walter's car, and Sidney's wife… Well Sidney. What news? Where are they?'

'Still in Truro, thank God. They haven't broken down after all. Lottie says they had a successful day, and a lovely meal but are too tired to drive back , – so they are going to make a night of it…well she didn't quite put it like that, – but she was very chuffed about being on television. I told her we forgot to switch on.'

'Shame on you, Sidney. Young Charlotte would have loved to know we saw her, – just wait till she gets home!'

'It is blowing great guns, – I'd better go out and tie up the gate. Can't trust my repair – I don't want it blowing over the cliff.'

'Leave it, Sidney, – leave it! You'll risk getting blown over the cliff yourself! It does happen, you know…'

'Can't let Walter down, Nan. He is taking such a pride in the place, isn't he Emmie? Mustn't lose a gate the moment his back is turned.'

My dear, dearest Emmie,

What can I write? What comfort can I be? I feel so helpless, – so separated, – not just in distance but in time, because, Emmie dear, I have only just heard. When I came back to my hotel this evening there was a brief note from Alec. He read about the tragedy in a newspaper, – only the bare facts, – and he was asking me what happened, obviously he thought I knew. We have always known everything about each other, and even now my reflex action was to pick up the telephone, like a fool, before I realised that this is the middle of your night, and I don't even know where you are now.

Emmie dear, I do share your grief, I am the only one who can, perhaps, yet I know how little comfort that can be. What an irony, Emmie, that after a lifetime of sharing the trivia of our lives there comes a real need to communicate and I am isolated in this, – I was going to say God-forsaken country, but that is far from true. God comes very strong in these parts, and through the most bizarre media, is second only to culture, it seems, which means that a writer from Oxford, England, is taken very seriously, which is the hell of a strain. But Emmie! What am I doing? Writing about myself! Forgive me and take it as a measure of my distress, dear, – longing to comfort you and not knowing how to begin. I am not even sure where you are now, unable to imagine if you would stay or go in the circumstances, – so I will send this to your home and get it into the post at once.

Please forgive this chaotic letter, and please write, Emmie, as soon as you feel able, – to Berkeley. My roaming in these vast plains lasts only another week, I have lost track of where I am, – every town looks alike. The organisation is adequate, but my God the post is slow.

Believe me, Emmie darling, to be ever your own

Janice.

Trevelgue Manor

Dearest Janice,

Your letter has arrived, – forwarded here, – and is comfort indeed, though it makes me shed more tears. The delay has helped, I am more composed now, – and it is such a relief that you already know. I don't feel I could break the news, even now. They have been shielding me from all those troubles, and now I must gather myself together. But I'm afraid I cannot write much, so forgive me, I will try, – try to tell you what happened, – and even to make a start I must find my way back into the world as it was when I last wrote, – another world! How lightly these phrases fall from one's pen, – until they acquire real meaning.

I can remember the day vividly, the last I can recall clearly, – a lovely sunny day, Carlotta and Walter waving so cheerily, starting off on their trip to a motor-rally, as I told you. And here a quiet pleasant day, when I had a chance to write to you because Mr Elliot had some business letters to answer. And then when I looked out there he was mending the cliff gate, which he didn't manage very well and came in to tell Nan, – and they saw the car-show on television, but I missed it, – and he made a joke about Lottie making up to the interviewer, and Nan scolded him....My memory begins to blur, but I remember that Carlotta telephoned later in the evening. We thought they had broken down, – but it was only to tell us that she and Walter were too tired to drive back and were staying the night in Truro.

We were so happy to hear that they were not on the road, because a great gale had sprung up, Mr Elliot – I cannot call him Sidney now, – said he was afraid his repair to the gate would not hold for long and he must go out to secure it with rope. Nan warned him that it was dangerous to go near the cliff edge, that he could easily be blown off himself, – but he went anyway.

I saw Nan looking at me, and I felt myself looking at her as if we both had a terrible premonition, though we said nothing. However it turned out to be only the fear of the moment because Mr Elliot came in safe and sound and put our premonitions to shame.

He was very cheerful at having saved the gate, having caught it just in time, he said, and was even happier at having been reprieved, as he put it, from having to go out and deal with a broken-down car on such a foul night. So Nan and I went to bed happily, our premonitions calmed.

On the following morning the weather was atrocious, with a high wind and heavy driving rain. Mr Elliot had listened to the weather forecast and said that Cornwall was in the centre of a depression, so little hope of a clearance all day. Well I suppose that Carlotta and Walter decided that they could not hang about in Truro indefinitely. The car hood was supposed to be watertight and I dare say that they considered restricted visibility to be a nuisance rather than a hazard, – but that obviously was what caused the accident, – the car ran off the road. I still can't really believe it happened, – it is like describing a nightmare. Would that it were!

A man driving in the following car said that they were descending a steep hill, and when the Delage drove straight through an open gate instead of rounding a hairpin bend it looked, – according to this witness, – as if the driver knew where he was going. But then the car suddenly vanished out of sight which so puzzled him that after driving on a short distance he parked his car, and in spite of the rain walked back to investigate. The Delage had crashed over a cliff – into an old quarry in fact. Even then the man could not rid himself of his first impression, – that the driver of the Delage had intended to drive through the gateway. It is perhaps inevitable that any witness, shaken by a terrible experience, cannot be shaken from his first impression, however mistaken, and it is only natural that he should keep repeating the first thought that came into his mind. Which this man did, causing much additional distress since then.

We shall never know what happened. I suspect that the screen-wiper failed and Walter was momentarily blinded. The police reported that the car had probably skidded on over the wet grass down the slight incline under its own impetus. The driver and passenger were killed instantly. I can't stop thinking of those last moments. You may be surprised that I can write, – I surprise myself. But what a relief it is to unburden to you so much which I cannot speak of here.

They have been so kind trying to shield me from the horror of those first days. They hid the newspapers and I let them believe they had succeeded, and in this way perhaps we somehow managed to comfort each other, – but I did manage to find and read the account in The Western Morning News.

When the police telephoned about the accident Mr Elliot would not let me go with him. He looked very shaken so Nan and I feared the worst, and although we still had hope the hours of waiting were terrible. Sophie was having one of her fretful days and her continual plaint that Charlotte never came was hard to bear. Yet it was comforting in a way, being so familiar, making it seem impossible that Carlotta would not once again come into the room filling it with her optimism and little plans, and with poor Walter too.

But when Mr Elliot entered the house and Nan and I rushed out to meet him we could see the worst in his face, he looked like death himself. 'Fatal…'he said, 'both…' He could hardly speak and Nan took him in her arms, which I longed to do.

I went back to Sophie whose fretfulness had suddenly turned to a weird keening, – which has made me wonder if perhaps in a moment of lucidity she had overheard and knew. But whatever her brain might have understood briefly it refused to accept and she continues as before, – so you can imagine, Jan, that her expectations and complaints are equally impossible to bear.

The funeral was planned to be quiet and the intervening days passed in a kind of numbed disbelief, – which still persists, – with the inquest, which I did not have to attend. But totally unforeseen questions needed answering and deciding.

How little one is prepared for sudden death, how shocking the questions, however gently asked, about what is to be done. Would Walter have wished his body to be taken home? Well I felt, – indeed I knew, that he would have no such wish. As for myself the thought of such a journey, – returning to the empty house at all filled me with dread. And what were Walter's wishes concerning burial or cremation? Well this was clear, we had both decided on cremation in the days when we could not really imagine it applying to us. Oh Jan, how laughingly we had dealt with that very topic only a few weeks before, when Carlotta said she would wish her ashes to be scattered from the cliff tops, and Mr Elliot made a joke as usual. Poor Carlotta had become quite hysterical when burying was mentioned, – but even then she was thinking of her mother.

So Carlotta and Walter were both to be cremated according to their wishes, though they had not wished to die. A joint funeral was arranged and we never gave a thought to the stir and scandal this would cause

In the meanwhile Peter, Mr Elliot's son by his first wife who died, rang up to say he would attend the funeral, and as he replaced the receiver Mr Elliot sighed, and said to Nan, 'Peter is coming, and Meryl too. So it looks, Nan, that I am to be accepted back into the fold.' He spoke with unusual bitterness and sighed again.

Very little was ever spoken of Peter, which had surprised me until Nan confided that he didn't approve of his father's second marriage, which was Meryl's influence, she thought, because Peter seemed an easy-going fellow like his father. But Meryl only too obviously disapproved of Charlotte, – from jealousy no doubt, Nan said, and then there was the money, of course.

But the funeral, Jan! The dreariness of cremation. We got through the service somehow, it was short enough, God knows. I suppose they do their best. And then suddenly, unexpectedly, shockingly, the coffins were moving, gradually disappearing behind curtains, – we knew where, and Nan and I clung to each other, we were all three terribly affected. These gruesome mechanics, pathetically attempting the dignity of ritual seemed to compound the tragedy. As we came away I did not notice who else was in the chapel, I could not see for tears.

Carlotta's ashes were to be scattered from the cliffs as she had wished, at a point she had specially loved, not far from the house. Mr Elliot had asked me what should be done for Walter, and I had suggested that perhaps his ashes could be scattered there at the same time, and Mr Elliot said that if I had no other preference he agreed that would be best.

If we could have foreseen, Jan, the family disapproval, how the press would seize on this, – what would be their interpretation, – we might have been restrained. But I am glad we could not foresee. I cannot regret the decision. I could not bear to think of Walter being lonely. I think, – I know, – that he really loved Carlotta and I'm not surprised, she gave him back his youth. You will understand now why it is such a relief to write to you. I cannot speak of it here, – and I could not have spoken of it on the telephone. I do not think they guess.

There was a surprising ceremony for the scattering of the ashes, – surprising to me at least. If I had not been too dazed to think at all I would have expected an entirely private happening. Carlotta had so revelled in her wild empty cliff-tops, especially the quiet of the evening when the few cliff walkers had disappeared, – though how Mr Elliot and Nan and I could ever have braved ourselves to do the scattering, I had not begun to imagine.

So perhaps it was just as well that the local clergyman, an earnest young priest who obviously rejoiced in the ritual of his calling, decided that cremation was not properly the funeral's end, and had persuaded Mr Elliot that a few prayers should be said at the cliff edge. The result was that quite a crowd gathered, headed by an assortment of the media, – and it has occurred to me since that this perhaps, after all, was just what Carlotta would have desired. It is difficult to tell, – but for all her love of solitude she did have a sense of occasion.

I was in the lowest ebb of sadness, numbed, as I said before, as we stumbled over the rough grass of the cliff-top together, Nan and Mr Elliot and I, following the firm stride of the young priest to the spot which had been chosen. It was a calm sunny evening, the fatal depression which had caused the accident had passed and after dragging cold north winds in its wake had been replaced by fair weather.

The young priest spoke his words. Mr Elliot took Nan's arm and mine as the remains of poor Carlotta and Walter were carried on the breeze. Gulls were wheeling and gliding and soaring on the light air, just as Carlotta had said she longed to do.

The impression of lightness was uplifting, and suddenly I felt calmed, soothed, almost happy, my vision cleared and I began to see about me with the utmost clarity, – the sheen on the grass, the dwarf foliage glistening in the sun. And then I looked further and encountered a hard hostile stare from Meryl, a stare caught unawares and hastily replaced with a devout funeral expression which still emanated disapproval.

She emanated middle-age too, though she was half a generation younger than Carlotta. And there was an old wild-looking woman, weeping uncontrollably. 'Why it is Athelie!' cried Nan, and ran to console her.

Then as soon as the ceremony was over the reporters began to press upon us and Mr Elliot whispered that we must get away. He told them to talk to his son, and forced a way through to Nan and Athelie. Peter hung back, and it was the daughter-in-law who kept the reporters engaged while we made our escape to the house. I could hear her talking to them as we went, in a high-pitched voice, giving tongue as it seemed to me, I suppose I was a bit hysterical. However she kept them at bay successfully and the clamour died away behind us.

Nan tried to persuade Athelie to come inside with us, but she had a car waiting and refused to venture into the house. I felt so sorry, watching her being driven away alone. The encounter had happened so unexpectedly, I have felt sad for her, and curious ever since.

Meryl and Peter joined us after a while, – no doubt the reporters had to meet their deadlines. Such questions they had asked, Meryl said, she had hardly known how to answer. Of course she had foreseen that such a funeral was bound to cause comment, and sure enough their questions had been loaded with innuendo. And had we realised we were being televised? The cameras were on her all the time, Meryl said. She had done her best to be as discreet as possible in the circumstances, – but it was really an impossible situation and had been very embarrassing.

She made us feel apologetic, filling our sorrow with uneasiness, our unhappiness with doubt. Nan and I tried to quieten her with tea, which she seemed to enjoy, helping herself to quantities of saffron cake spread with clotted cream, eating it absentmindedly while talking, and it was soon evident that far from being put out she had enjoyed being the centre of publicity.

After tea was cleared she looked at her watch and ordered Peter to switch on the television so that we should not miss the local news. Peter, who was obviously used to obeying such little commands, did as he was bid, forgetting perhaps that he was not even in his father's house. I saw Nan and Mr Elliot looking at each other and then at me, both with the same concern that I might be distressed. We were so taken aback that I replied with half a smile to indicate that I did not mind, we had none of us smiled since the accident so I suppose this reassured them.

We watched uncomfortably, there were several items of news with figures that seemed like puppets on the screen, no longer of interest to any of us. Meryl's impatience was obvious, she kept clucking about her own interview, her ordeal on the cliff-top, commiserating with people who were in the public eye, and thankful she wasn't royalty, never able to escape, poor things.

Nan sat quietly, concealing impatience of quite another kind, and Mr Elliot sat as one frozen. In desperate need of comfort, mourning Carlotta, I believe he also mourned that he could not love his daughter-in-law. Have you noticed, Jan, that people on the whole wish to like their in-laws? But this cannot always be managed. I didn't get the impression that Peter is unhappily nagged, but there is no doubt he is lost to his father.

Then came the announcement of the funeral, giving my heart pause, and a moment of suffocation. The news was presented discreetly, with genuine regret and, full marks to the BBC, we were spared the Meryl interview. They flashed back first to scenes from the motor-show, which I had missed before. Oh Jan! To see the Delage again, gleaming in the sunshine, – and Carlotta looking so happy, so beautiful, ageless, – and Walter so proud, it simply wasn't possible to believe them dead. And though my heart increased its beat most painfully, strangely enough it felt flooded with happiness rather than sorrow. And then the scene changed to the cliff-tops, the priest in silhouette, gulls wheeling against a back-drop of sea and sky, and three mourners bent with grief, – unbelievably us, standing slightly to one side.

There were no close-ups, no prying into our distress, – and mercifully no Meryl.

The picture faded and another item followed. Mr Elliot got up and left the room abruptly, slamming the door behind him. I saw that tears were streaming down Nan's face and I reached out to hold her hand. I supposed their reaction was different from mine because they had seen the pictures before, while Carlotta and Walter were still alive, – and to watch them again, followed by the scene on the cliffs, – you can imagine how unbearable.

Meryl was clearly miffed that her interview had been ignored. She gave a kind of snort which made her husband nervous. 'Shall I switch off now?' he asked, addressing himself to Nan. Nan stood up, her grief choked down by a sudden flare of anger. 'Just as your wife wishes, Peter,' she said, 'Please feel quite at home. If you will excuse me I must go and attend to Sophie.'

Nan left the room without looking back and I got up to follow her without apology, they didn't seem to notice if I was there or not and Meryl started talking before I had properly closed the door. I heard her saying, 'I always told you that this foolish obsession of your father's would end in scandal!'

Well, Jan, you may be sure that instead of closing the door I stayed to listen. 'The shameless pretentious flirt!' said Meryl, 'Making an exhibition of herself with that other man, – and then staying out all night. No wonder they had an accident, they were probably still drunk, the pair of them…'

Peter was muttering something half-audible, rather apologising for his father than defending him, it seemed. 'That is all very well,' said Meryl, 'But now there is this other woman, a mere acquaintance, behaving as if she is family, – your father ought to be ashamed of himself...'

I was too stunned to listen further. It came upon me like a thunderbolt, Jan, this revelation of what other people could possibly think. I had heard too much and fled upstairs to Nan. But of course even then I could not speak to her of what I had heard. You are the only person I can tell, – and what a relief it is to write. I do not think they guess the extent of Meryl's jealousy.

She left with Peter on the following morning and reported to us on the telephone later that they had encountered some 'gentlemen of the Press' snooping round the house but had succeeded in getting rid of them. For this we were supposed to be grateful, but if you ask me Merryl was a gift to the reporters as we realised when the tabloids caught up the story.

I can hear Sophie's bell, – she has taken to staying in bed lately, – almost as if she knows, – I wonder? I had better see what she wants – to save Nan climbing the stairs.

'Would you believe it, Nan, I've just seen off another of those prying bastards…with a camera!'

'Surely not reporters still?'

'Probably some ghoulish sightseer. But whenever will they leave us alone? It's not as if we were public figures –or weren't – until this monstrous invasion of our privacy…'

'Sidney dear, don't distress yourself!'

'I'm not distressed. I simply feel I could murder them! For me it is just exasperating…but for Emmie!'

'Emmie has more sense than you give her credit for.'

'Well, I'd just like to get my hands on the reporter who sparked off these absurd love-pact and death-tryst theories. As if Walter would have deliberately driven his precious motor over a cliff! You haven't any doubts about that, have you Nan?'

'Now you are being absurd, Sidney. If Charlotte had any romantic notion of ending their lives by driving over a cliff she would never have chosen the quarry, – it has been used as a rubbish dump for years!'

'By Jove, Nan, – you have a cogent argument there. So what do you make of the alternative theory that I tampered with the brakes… out of jealousy?'

'My dear Sidney! As much credence as I give to Aunt Jessie's disapproval.'

'Ah, so you've thought of that too? The case of the scandalised ghost! Luckily the Press haven't heard about Aunt Jessie or we'd have a pack of ghost-hunters about the place. But with a scandalised live daughter-in-law meddling in one's affairs who needs ghosts?'

'Meryl's presence was a disaster. All her hypocritical talk of being tactful with reporters!'

'There is no doubt she started their sly insinuations about partner-swapping. Thank God Emmie hasn't seen the papers. Of course I knew that Lottie had a bit of a thing for Walter as well as his car, which amused me at first, though I began to see her point... I became quite fond of old Walter myself in the end, one couldn't have wished her ashes mingled with those of a nicer chap...'

'Sidney, for goodness sake!'

'Do you think the ceremony on the cliff was a mistake, Nan? I thought poor Lottie would like some sort of formal send-off...and who could have foreseen the Press cooking up such a romantic interpretation, for God's sake, and with such malicious undertones. What else could we have done? Brought the ashes home and kept them on the mantle-piece – and called the cleric back after the hullabaloo died down?'

'Sidney dear!'

'Besides the weather was perfect that day... we could hardly have hoped for better conditions...'

'You will have to watch your words, Sidney, or your brave attempts at cynicism will distress that good creature upstairs. Emmie is sensible, – but sensitive too, – and very unhappy. And you don't fool me, my dear, I know how deeply you feel. I know that the light has gone from your life...'

'The lightness, Nan, Lottie was the lightness of my life, – gone now, – gone. I don't feel that being accepted back by my family would have compensated, – which is unlikely now after what has happened, – and just as well as far as I'm concerned. I was incensed from the moment that unmitigated bitch ordered the television to be switched on. Though I'm glad we saw it, Nan. I think Lottie would have approved. It was just what she asked for, remember? Poor dear Lottie, she had no thought of dying so soon. But how would it have ended, I wonder, Nan, if the affair had lingered on?'

'You mean with Walter? They were a couple of innocents, Sidney.'

'Innocence is fragile, Nan.'

'You may be right, but a brain also can be fragile, – console yourself if you can, dear. You only have to look at Sophie...and

Athelie too, for that matter. Ah, there is Sophie's bell now, – we don't want her disturbing Emmie.'

Nan came up to look after Sophie and wouldn't let me disturb myself. She knew I was writing to you and told me not to hurry. Dear Nan, I have been deceiving her in a way, deceiving them both. In fact we have all been deceiving each other.

As I told you, there was an account of the accident in the Western Morning News, and then a full report of the inquest, and a restrained and sympathetic account of the ceremony on the cliffs which has since captured the public imagination. The newspaper was tactfully hidden each day, but I managed to find it anyway. Sorrow itself made me restless, athirst for news and hungry for every crumb of information, – and after Meryl's complaint of being pestered by reporters I guessed there must be more.

The women who come in to work bring the Mirror and The Sun each day. They swap them over the coffee break and discuss the stories, and it was a joke among us that Mr Elliot made a habit of going into the kitchen to read sensational snippets and enjoy a laugh with them too. The women work around the house together and you can see that this made it easy for me to creep into the kitchen and have a look through the papers. But would you believe it, from a few words Mr Elliot let slip this morning I began to suspect that we were all doing the same thing. Which had never occurred to me when the household was so hushed and subdued and laughter over the coffee break a thing of the past. And what is more, if I had suspected I would have wanted to hide the papers too, – to prevent the others reading what I read.

Poor dear Nan who was always so loyal to Carlotta, and Mr Elliot wandering round like a lost soul, looking so angry and brooding, – I can see why now. We must all have had the same compulsion to know all, no matter how twisted the truth or how hurtful the insinuation. How little we think, Janice, when we read sensational news, of the distress caused to innocent relatives.

The story had grown out of plain fact to begin with when one reporter who was in more of a hurry to get his story off than to check facts was misled by a slip of the tongue on local television when Walter was referred to as Mr Elliot. So one London daily reported that both Elliots had died in the crash, and this resulted in poor Peter receiving a number of letters of condolence, which so exasperated Meryl that eventually she packed them up and sent them to her father-in-law with an angry cover-note. Can you imagine anyone being so cruel? It just shows how jealous she was of Carlotta, as I told you.

Mr Elliot received the packet at breakfast this morning and exploded when he opened it, – and it was from what he let slip then that I realised we had all been reading the popular press. He started to make a joke about his 'obituaries' but then he caught Nan's eye and remembered me, – and poor Walter, – and Carlotta of course, and was suddenly silent. Your letter had just arrived too, Janice, we were all choked with emotion and none of us ate a thing. In fact I have gone quite thin in these last two weeks, – which would have made me happy in happier times, – oh dear, I still cannot believe that it has all really happened and those happy times are gone for ever.

As to the rumour growing up you can imagine that the accident coming immediately after the publicity of the motor-show aroused widespread sympathy. And then the evidence of the eye-witness at the inquest was reported at length, – but there is no doubt that the joint funeral and the dramatic cliff ceremony really caught the public imagination and gave such romantic ideas to the Press. Of course it could not be romance without being something of a scandal too, – helped I am sure by Meryl's hints. Obviously scandal is even more newsworthy than romance and when the news-hounds began to try to unravel the story backwards the most astonishing versions appeared in the tabloids.

The reporter who had mistaken the name gained a head start by having to retract – which he very cleverly did to his own advantage, not to mention that he had certainly encountered Meryl. "It had come to light," he wrote, – as if the fact had been concealed in the first place, "that the owner of the car was not Mrs Elliot's husband, but a friend whom she accompanied to numerous motor-shows and trips abroad."

The reporter said that he had been assured by a near relative that they were 'just good friends' Meryl's words, obviously, which couldn't have made her meaning clearer. And to pass herself off as 'a near relative' when she wasn't remotely related to either of them!

And I fear that in the neighbourhood generally it had been noted that Walter usually walked with Carlotta and Mr Elliot walked with me, which gave rumour to 'partner swapping!' Really Jan we never gave thought to local opinion and I don't suppose the locals did either until it was suggested to them. And what's more the papers raked up some archival photos which we hadn't seen before, of Carlotta and Walter together at the Blenheim show, which gave me another shock to be sure, – and once again of delight seeing them still alive and so happy in the sunshine.

The reporters were not dismayed by the paucity of fact which allowed them to speculate with those diabolical questions with which they avoid libel. Bizarre questions like "LOVERS' LEAP?' – which at first glance didn't strike me as possibly referring to us. The idea of a romantic tryst with death arose from speaking to the witness of the accident who was only too willing to repeat his first impression , – that Walter had intended to drive through the gate. I know this witness did not wish to mislead, that was made clear at the inquest, it was simply his first thought, and that was enough for the Press.

And this brought a counter-speculation. If no leap was intended why had the car run over the edge? Why had its brakes failed? The local garage owner admitted that a cable was found to be broken, but in his opinion it had been severed in the crash.

So from a cunning juxtaposition of statement and question there were hints of sinister possibilities, – a romantic death-wish on one side, and on the other malicious intent, – I cannot write more, it is all too ghastly.

And I felt so alone at that time, Jan, never guessing that anyone else knew. Now that I believe they did I feel better. We must have this out. And writing to you has cleared my mind. I did not think I could even begin – but how I have been carried along in the flood which poured out of me once started!

You write that you wonder where I am, saying that you cannot imagine me going or staying in these circumstances. And neither can I. I cannot yet visualise where I shall be in the future. Of course it has been unthinkable to abandon Nan just yet, – though in fact it is she who is our strength, while Mr Elliot and I drift about the house like lost souls, – homeless bodies, – because where else is there now for either of us to go?

'So there you are, Emmie, reading the popular press. What rubbish have they printed today?'

'It is over, Nan, – completely forgotten, – now that they have done their worst.'

'We shall not forget so soon, my dear, though time must ease the pain.'

'As long as it can be shared in future, Nan. I have been so touched by your care, – but the loneliness of being protected! And I had to know, – I thought I was the only one who read these papers, – which made me feel lonelier still –until yesterday, – at breakfast, – when I guessed...'

'Emmie dear, how changed you are since yesterday! Your friend's letter seems to have brought you back to life. And Meryl's cruel note has had the same effect on Sidney. He is recovering a strength of purpose which will not be welcomed by her I think.'

'Nan tells me you have been reading the papers, Emmie.'

'It is true, – I have been reading all I could lay hands on, and thought you didn't know...'

'And she tells me you were lonely.'

'Yes, I did feel so solitary, being unable to talk to you, or even to Nan. But it was better so, I can see that now. It would have been unbearable if we all had known what the others knew and had all been worrying about each other's distress, – oh dear, I do get so mixed up with words...'

'I cannot bear to think that you were lonely, Emmie.'

'Ah but the comfort now I'm not!'

'Emmie dear! I feel such an urgent need to care for you…if you could think of letting me…We seem to rub along together so well, don't we? Of course I know I can never replace…You don't have to say anything yet…I realise it is too soon…and anyway we'd have to wait awhile until our fame dies down. But it would round off the scandal nicely, don't you think?'

'I…oh dear…'

'Emmie darling! You are laughing! Come Nan, come and listen to this! Come and scold me again for making jokes, – I've made Emmie laugh! Which is too soon, and improper and all that, – and Meryl would never approve…Oh God, now she is crying…'

'Emmie dear! Don't distress yourself. Whatever is he blathering now?'

'Emmie is going to marry me Nan! That is to say, I think she is…if I can manage to persuade her of course…and if she can bring herself to call me Sidney, – just the once…'

'Oxford 98245'

'Janice! How good to hear your voice at last…'

'My dear, I've only just got in! Emmie dear, how are you now? And where are you?'

'Still at Trevelgue. Oh Janice, we have been so sad, I never thought I'd survive to begin with. Thank God you know it all already…'

'Emmie darling, I was so distressed, – I've been so worried about you…'

'But now, Jan, – listen, – I've got the most unbelievable news…which must be secret for a while. You are the only person I can tell…'

END

TWO MORE FICTITIOUS TALES

A WINE MERCHANT

James Hibbard, of Hibbard & Tapley, Importers of Fine Wines, was an unhappy and a frightened man. His terrestrial affairs flourished, he had a prosperous business, an affectionate wife, and to ease his travel to Continental vineyards had just acquired an old farmhouse near London Airport. But Hibbard's unhappiness, not to mention fright, was extra-terrestrial, beyond his control The aircraft which had been carrying him to France had been forced to turn round before reaching the Channel, and was limping back to Heathrow.

Poor Hibbard, now living only ten minutes by car from Terminal 2, had already been trapped for nearly five hours in the Departure Lounge before the plane managed to get airborne. When eventually it was clear that he could not arrive in time to enjoy the superb Chateau dinner he telephoned his host. 'Ah, je suis désolé!' exclaimed M. Joret, 'Mais l'aéroport de Londres est toujours en grève!' Hibbard felt more than desolate with his gastric juices turning to bile, but as he hoped to clinch a good Joret vintage he did not explain that the present delay was caused by French Air-controllers manifesting discontent.

Hibbard returned from the telephone to find his seat occupied, the floor strewn with tourist bodies and struggling children. The bars were besieged by queues and it was past ten o'clock before he was able to settle himself in a window seat over the starboard wing of the aircraft. A heavy man lurched into the seat beside him belching oaths as he grappled with his seat-belt and then, overcome by the long wait in the bar, sank into drunken sleep.

The plane began its painful lumbering along the runway, accelerating until the tyres seemed about to explode. Relief coming at last when the aircraft entered its natural element with a surge of power which seized Hibbard by the small of his back, wrapping the seat firmly around his kidneys in a moment of exhilaration. James felt safer in the air, although touchdown, quite the most scary moments of this abominable mode of transport, had still to be survived

He switched off his light and watched the glittering world tilting away beneath him as the plane lifted through the luminous soft underbelly of cloud and climbed on into dark mist. Hibbard was wishing he had let his partner, Brian Tapley, go on this trip. Brian no doubt had deserved to go, he had been the first to suspect that the modest Chateau might harvest a superior vintage. But Hibbard's wife, Constance, had advised against it. 'Monsieur Joret might be hurt if you send your junior partner,' she had said.

As the aircraft emerged through the last billows into a silvery moonlit cloudscape it banked steeply, seeming to swerve, and while the wing tilted beneath him James thought he saw a piece of metal spin away. His first reaction was increased exasperation and then horror struck him as another small piece fell away. No one else had noticed. He lifted a hand and caught the attention of the airhostess, she came and bent towards him. James whispered to her, smiling with an idiot smile quite beyond his control. The girl smiled back fleetingly and went forward to the cockpit.

After a short interval a voice announced that the plane must return to Heathrow. The passengers were instructed to fasten their seatbelts and there was a rustle of outrage but no panic. The poor overburdened French Air-controllers were obviously responsible for the turn round.

But James knew. And his unhappiness now was nothing to his fright. What advantage to him now that his seat was next to an emergency door over the wing when the plane was disintegrating in flight! But the air-hostess, walking calmly in the aisle to check that seat-belts were fastened, smiled cheerfully at Hibbard as if parts dropping off a plane were an everyday occurrence, which indeed, to recall recent news items it would seem they were.

The plane began its endless cautious descent and Hibbard sat stiff in his seat with fright, his brain lively with apprehension. It took several minutes to burn to death. Why the hell hadn't he let Brian Tapley go on this trip! Not that he wished Brian any harm, he simply wasn't ready to die himself, let alone to suffer. And poor Connie left a widow!

Brian of course would take care of her, – and, no doubt, console her! Ah death where is thy sting? Where indeed? Poised ready to strike! Words which had consoled James when intoned over someone else's grave were of little comfort when death's sting was imminent, ready to take stab at himself.

The rictus of smile playing over Hibbard's face like summer lightning flashed on and off quite beyond his control.

Constance Hibbard was an unhappy and a frightened woman, alone on a summer night in the house which was to have been the delight of her life, – unhappy because she had not expected to be afraid.

Their friends had shuddered at the isolation of the place, set in the few remaining fields of Hillingdon. 'Solitude does not frighten me,' Constance had told them. And grim warnings were uttered about moving in with building work in progress before locks and alarms were fitted. But the Hibbards had been happy camping out with the bulk of their furniture stowed away.

The evenings were idyllic as they wandered in the wilderness of garden watching deepening reflections in the reedy pond. There was a distant hum of traffic but no sound of the aircraft noise which makes life hideous from Windsor to Kew because Hillingdon lies parallel to the runways. James would say over again, 'The peace, Connie, you cannot put a price on it!' And Brian Tapley liked the house, coming to eat with them on Sundays, helping James to saw fallen trees for the wood stack.

Brian was really rather a dear, though James did not approve of his manners, let alone his business projects. Brian, managing their small branch near St Katherine's Dock, had introduced a Video library and sold wine in plastic cartons with taps. James disapproved, 'When they buy a bottle they've got to drink it up,' he said.

But Brian's customers enjoyed having wine on tap, kept running dry and coming back for more, especially the women, Brian told them, who would slink in mid-week to buy another carton without the old man knowing. 'Our firm is not in the business of turning wives into alcoholics,' James replied, looking ferociously at Connie who was laughing. Constance was astonished, but stopped laughing.

Surely the old idiot could not be jealous of Brian! But when Brian, who also enjoyed the Joret cuisine, wished to go on that mission, she thought it wiser not to take his part. And so James had gone and now Connie wished she had persuaded him to let Brian go instead.

Earlier Constance had come tired from gardening to a bare room where two basket chairs faced a neglected television perched on its one leg. She sat drowsily watching a documentary on urban crime until a unnerving description of rape made her flash over to ITV where the picture was dark, dimly showing a man creeping through dense shrubbery towards a lighted window. He reached the window, his head outlined against it. And within, sitting at ease, unaware of peril, a lone woman was watching television. Constance leapt to her feet snapping off the set, plunging the room in darkness.

Moonlight shining through the uncurtained window established a patch of light on the bare floor and illuminated the tangle of shrubs beyond the terrace. Connie could no longer persuade herself that the isolated house was safe from city crime. The front door was locked, never used because it was easier to enter through the half-built garden room where the builders draped the hole with plastic at the end of the day.

James had taken the car and Connie felt trapped with rapists lurking in the undergrowth around her. Cloud darkened the moon and too frightened to switch on a light she decided to go upstairs where she could not be overlooked, leaving a light in the kitchen to show that the household was still awake.

Constance lay on the bed trying to read. The night was quiet, the murmur of traffic remote, and in spite of fear she drifted into sleep, – drifting into nightmare in which a telephone was ringing, and with nightmare knowledge she knew that a thief was checking that the house was empty and safe to burgle.

She was struggling against nightmare odds to get to the telephone before the ringing stopped, – dragging leaden limbs, trying to force her eyelids open…. Then she awoke to hear that the bell was indeed ringing, – but for how long? Impelled by the influence of nightmare she rushed down the stairs to reach it before it stopped. But as she crossed the bare room another danger struck her, – that a woman's voice might well be an invitation to burgle, – or even worse to rape.

She picked up the receiver, automatically announcing the number, and then had a brilliant idea. She shouted over her shoulder: 'I've got it, darling! Don't bother coming down….' There was a click at the end of the line and the dialling tone replaced silence, Constance sank onto a chair wondering if her ploy had worked.

Constance continued to sit, not knowing what else to do, afraid to return to bed and nightmare although it was past midnight. The telephone bell was rendered mute, its receiver purring softly like a kitten in her lap. The illuminated clock counted minutes slowly, five, ten, – fifteen, and then suddenly there was a slight noise on the terrace. Someone was creeping round the house.

James Hibbard had himself driven home as fast as the taxi-driver could be urged to drive. He had escaped death after a nightmare descent and touchdown.

Unlike the enviable drunk beside him his own body had been rigid with fear, every muscle taught, each bone brittle ready to snap like a matchstick. But the damaged plane survived, had jolted along the runway to pull up safely, and as he queued to descend the gangway Hibbard was invited into the cockpit to be congratulated on his cool behaviour. He knew that fear had paralysed his capacity to panic, and even in the euphoria of relief guessed that he was being separated from chat with the other passengers and flattered into discretion.

But the flattery was gratifying, and so were the offers of help pressed upon him. He refused food, hotel accommodation or a car home, but as he passed through the terminal he decided to let his wife know of his miraculous escape and heroic behaviour, and to ask her besides to have something ready to eat.

He dialled their number and heard Connie repeating it, and then, – unbelievably she was shouting to someone else in the house: 'I've got it, darling! Don't bother coming down…'

This second shock did not paralyse Hibbard. He slammed down the receiver and without stopping to collect his car streaked out of the terminal and leapt into the nearest taxi. 'Drive as fast as you can,' he shouted, 'this is a matter of life and death!'

And whose life was now in danger he had not the slightest doubt. That snake Brian! His mind seethed in chaotic ferment. No wonder Connie had persuaded him to go instead of Brian! No wonder she claimed to be happy alone! Alone indeed!

As they reached the end of his drive Hibbard said, 'Stop here. I will walk the rest of the way,' He jumped out and thrust a fifty-pound note into the man's hand. 'Keep the change!' he shouted and disappeared up the winding drive. The driver examined the note suspiciously, disinclined to trust a crazy chap who was first of all in such a hurry and then wanted to walk, but the note seemed genuine so he shrugged his shoulders and drove away. A taxi-driver's life is filled with unfinished stories.

James crept quietly round the house to catch his wife and partner in flagrante. He passed the front door and reached the plastic curtain, dislodging a brick as he pulled it aside. He put his hand around the opening and switched a light, – to find his wife standing in front of him, guilty, terrified! And then in a moment she was in his arms sobbing with relief.

A little later they were sitting at the kitchen table, each repeating their stories of fright. James, who was eating scrambled egg, was already taking for granted the miraculous gift of life and felt somewhat peeved that Connie did not properly appreciate his coolness in the face of danger. She simply could not stop giggling over his reaction to the phone call. 'I love you, James,' she said, getting up to give him another hug.

'But darling, of course I knew there was some simple explanation,' lied her husband, – silently mourning the unconfessed change from his fifty pound note, – and well aware that this was the kind of marital joke which would take some living down.

MURDER PREMEDITATED

Mrs Langdon came upon her husband dead in his bed one morning. The living being who had shared her forty years of married life transmogrified overnight into a gruesome corpse with its jaw locked open in a hideous grimace. The strength drained from her legs and she sank down on to the chair over which he had thrown his clothes, anaesthetised by shock, unaware that his trouser-buckle was biting into her plump posterior.

Her husband had long been a sorry sight in the morning, a sodden snoring hulk, or an ill-tempered figure shapeless with sleep shambling to the bathroom. But during the past months while a plan for the perfect undetectable murder swirled in Mrs Langdon's brain, – the plan for two deaths which would free her from an alcoholic husband and a dotty mother-in-law, she gave no thought to the sheer horror of coming upon a dead body, and now, even in her numbed state she was dimly aware that had they shared the same bed such a crime could never have been contemplated.

Her husband's savage hangovers had been the private face of a convivial extrovert, popular with his friends, reckoned to be a fond husband and, – as poor Mrs Langdon knew to her cost, – an exemplary son. A man whose testiness over expenditure and tight control of the purse strings ensured that life was arranged to his own convenience.

But the financial burdens which so irritated this exemplary husband were as nothing compared with the human burden which had fallen upon the wife and daughter-in-law, driving her beyond the limit of tolerance, towards the edge of sanity.

Twelve years earlier when his sister who had looked after their mother died unexpectedly Langdon had said, 'Well, of course, Mother will have to come to live with us, – though I fear it won't be for long. She is knocking eighty now and was always frail. Luckily she is very fond of you,' he added, looking at his wife – and having no doubt on which side the fondness was critical.

And when she first came to live with them the dowager had been very fond, secretly delighted with the change which liberated her from a daughter she had disliked into the care of the son she adored. For years she had been trapped by poverty in a dismal terrace house and was now reprieved from what had seemed a life sentence. Transported to a pretty bungalow and the bright social life of an overgrown village near London, and confident that she could domesticate her daughter-in-law into providing the cosseting she was used to.

Not since the birth of her son had she risen for breakfast. Then there had been servants to bring it to her bed. But a financial crash and her husband's death had forced the removal to a dismal house. Her daughter became the breadwinner, but the breakfasts in bed continued. Carrying breakfast on a tray is often preferable to having some people up and about, – as Mrs Langdon soon found when she inherited the task.

The older woman, looking weak and fragile as she sat up in bed, greeted her daughter-in-law with a sweet smile each morning. 'Ah, here is my breakfast! What a good little thing you are! But we mustn't let me get lazy. I'll be up betimes tomorrow.'

There was a disparaging tone to the endearment 'little thing' which she used to diminish all compliments. 'Ah, macaroni cheese for lunch again! What an economical little thing you are! This reminds me of the delectable cheese soufflés cook used to make…' When speaking of the past the dowager ignored her days of poverty, seeming to forget she ever had a daughter.

Soon after her arrival the mother celebrated her eightieth birthday by having her curls freshly gilded for the occasion and only admitting publicly to seventy. The daughter-in-law cooked delicious food for a party and was rewarded by a fond pat on the shoulder and praised in front of everyone as 'this clever little thing.'

Fondness and helplessness worked like a charm and little precedents were easily established with each small point easier to concede than to argue. It can't be for ever, thought young Mrs Langdon as the months passed, strengthening the stranglehold of habit. But when months grew into years, each expected to be the last, she was no longer surprised that the daughter had died before the mother. The wonder was that her poor sister-in law had lasted so long.

The dowager seemed content to have established her age at seventy and approached her ninetieth birthday with this figure firmly lodged in her mind, – together with the fear of being put into a home. 'As if we could afford such a luxury!' said Langdon to his wife. 'Nine hundred a week it costs at Meadowbank now. Not that she couldn't do with locking up,' he added, – he had to miss a round of golf that morning while his wife went to the dentist.

By then his mother needed constant supervision but Langdon was unable to claim an attendance allowance because he enjoyed the luxury of a full-time wife. The old lady had been suffering from strange little attacks, and each time she recovered, their G.P., an old crony of Langdon's would say reassuringly, 'In your wife's good hands she'll celebrate her hundredth birthday yet.'

'She'll see me out, I don't doubt,' replied Langdon gloomily.

'I'd ease up on the bottle if I were you, old man.'

And to young Mrs Langdon as she let him out of the front door he said, 'The old lady will do very well unless she gets a sudden shock. We need to look after the man of the house, – it would be fatal to her if anything happened to her son.'

'Yes of course,' answered the wife, but the medic would have been surprised at the scenario which his caution pictured in her mind. The unfettered life of her widowed friends whose day-trips to London and regular visits to health-farms made their widowed state seem wholly enviable.

But as the dowager's behaviour became more dotty her physical state steadied, and it did indeed look doubtful if either relative could survive her. Langdon consoled himself with whisky, drinking himself into oblivion in the evening, unable to control his temper in the morning, and for his wife, often kept on her feet by Doan's backache pills, despair was turning into desperation.

Then an outraged full-time wife took her claim for an attendance allowance to the European Court and won. Langdon benefited from the judgement and his wife looked forward to some relief. But her husband decided it would be prudent to save the allowance. 'Mother is not much trouble at the moment,' he said, 'and we may have to put her into Meadowbank yet. As it is we spend a fortune on staff.' This was for a gardener once a week and domestic help twice.

'But it would be nice to have someone in occasionally so that I could get away for the day'

'My dear, Mother would get confused having a stranger to look after her. You know I'm always ready to take care of her when you go out.'

So Mrs Langdon tried taking her husband at his word but soon found that planning a day out in London was very different from keeping an appointment with her dentist. There was such bad humour and commotion over arrangements that in the end she gave up. I am a weak cowardly fool, she told herself, admiring the wife who had taken her case to The Hague, and yet feeling that standing up in an International court was as nothing to standing up to constant ill-humour at home.

Her only reprieve was when her husband was out and old Mrs Langdon fell into a short catnap, out of which she always awoke with a start, asking for her son. 'Wherever is he? Isn't it time to get his lunch?'

'Mother, he is lunching at the golf-club, he told you.'

Or in the evening. 'Gracious me, is it dark already? Whatever can have happened to him?'

'He has gone to a meeting, Mother, he only just kissed you good-bye!'

Within half an hour the same questions would be asked again. But when the demented woman took to patrolling the kitchen in the small hours and rousing them from their beds to ask if dinner was ready Langdon lost patience and made his G.P. friend prescribe a sleeping draught. Which his mother was happy to take, delighting in any extra care, only wishing that her son should share it.

So it was that one day her daughter-in-law came upon her mixing a deadly potion for her son, adding to the draught which he now had to take to keep himself alive a whole bottle of that which made her sleep. The doctor was alerted again and replacement doses were locked up in the cabinet over Langdon's wash-basin, the key hidden out of his mother's reach.

But in this cupboard Langdon kept his own private medicine, a bottle of whisky for emergency, which happened each time he ran out of his usual supply, when the bottle was quietly emptied and replaced. Of course his wife knew very well that her husband stole his own whisky, and that in his drunken state he often left the cabinet door open so that his mother could easily get at the medicine. And this gave her the idea of the perfect undetectable murder. That she herself could administer the fatal dose, and everyone would think her mother-in-law had done it.

Young Mrs Langdon, seeing herself as a rich free widow, laughed a black laugh. But her husband's black mood the next morning soon knocked any humour out of the joke. He little guesses how easily it could be done, she thought to herself as the bathroom door slammed.

And as one black morning followed another a deadly resolve began to grow, each day adding another practical touch except for solving the problem of how to leave her mother-in-law's fingerprints on the glass instead of her own.

The plan became addictive like a drug, a familiar window through which could be seen a more comfortable world beyond. But the unutterable horror of finding a live husband turned into a grisly corpse never entered her mind.

Yet here at last the deed was accomplished. There was her husband dead in his bed, and there was the glass on the bedside table, exactly as she had planned.

Poor Mrs Langdon sat in a chaos of bewilderment and guilt, and into the horror came a nightmare fear. She was quite unable to recall how she had managed the fingerprints. And so she sat, her posterior anaesthetised, her mind chaotic, until at last a flash of common sense penetrated the chaos.

'But I didn't do it!' she said to herself. 'Of course I didn't do it! Or did I? –Could I have? Am I mad?' she asked herself, hardly knowing if she had really been mad enough to kill her husband, or simply mad enough to think so.

There was a slight noise in the passage, and just as Mrs Langdon had certainly not murdered her husband, so now her instinctive impulse was to rush to shield his mother from seeing her son so horribly dead, the shock of which would certainly kill her. But it was too late, her mother-in-law was already standing in the doorway, dressed in a lacy petticoat, thick winter stockings, feathered mules, and a garden-party hat.

She surveyed the scene and smiled fondly. 'Ah, so the dear boy did take his medicine,' she said, going to the bedside table and picking up the empty glass. Then she patted the corpse gently. 'A nice lie-in will do him good. Only he will sleep with his mouth open, just like his father...' And she wandered out of the room.

Young Mrs Langdon had a moment of hysterical relief, – now there could be no question about the finger-prints! 'Oh God, what am I thinking now!' she said aloud. Of course she had not killed her husband, – but almost unbelievably it seemed that her mother-in-law had. The mother had not only killed her son but had survived the shock of seeing him so horribly dead.

This her enfeebled brain would never accept, and the younger woman, struggling to her feet, saw herself doomed to go along with the deceit. The dead man would be everlastingly lunching at his club or attending some meeting after dark. With a curious stabbing pain in her bottom adding itself to the chronic pain in her back she went to the telephone in the hall, past the open door of the bedroom where the older widow was back in bed lying limply among the pillows. 'Do be a good little thing,' she croaked, 'and bring my breakfast just this once…I hope to feel stronger tomorrow…'

Just this once indeed! Tomorrow and tomorrow and tomorrow! 'I'll be with you in a minute,' shouted young Mrs Langdon as she lifted the receiver to call the doctor who had predicted that her husband's mother would live to be a hundred.

THE WIFE

(A true story)

Mrs Hanson drove her Ultimate Driving Machine into a hotel courtyard and parked under a pollarded plane tree, aching in joint and muscle after driving five hundred miles from the Channel coast. I must be getting old, she thought, tottering round to the back of the car to take a small suitcase from the boot.

The bag was wedged amongst a collection of domestic items, a folding bed, table and chairs, sleeping bag, pillow, towels, kettle, pot and frying pan, and a plastic bag overflowing with cutlery and a dish-mop. The sordid jumble made her smile, – it was this which probably saved her from being stripped to the skin or worse on entering France.

Mrs Hanson had driven off the ship at seven o'clock that morning, a lone woman in an expensive car, used to travelling alone while her husband was at sea in command of a super-tanker the size of a football pitch.

She felt decidedly scruffy after a night on board and it did not cross her mind that she looked interesting enough to arouse suspicion from the demoralised remnants of Customs. But two men of sterner character, a drug squad perhaps, were also on watch and one stepped forward to signal her aside while the other requested her to descend to open the boot. 'I have nothing to declare,' she exclaimed, lifting the boot lid, ashamed at having to reveal such a sordid muddle. But the sight of bedclothes and cooking equipment brought a snort of disappointment from the official. 'Huh! Campeur!' he exclaimed in disgust, and Mrs Hanson was set free, rather cheered at having been separated from respectable tourists, and chuckling to herself as she drove.

How her husband would laugh when she told him! Campeur indeed! No more camping for them! Never again for them the hammering of tent pegs into solid rock at midnight! No more waking drenched with water under a collapsing tent in a thunderstorm! The purpose of her present journey was to keep an appointment with the Notary to take possession of a charming pièd a terre on the Atlantic coast of France, and the equipment in the car was for camping out within her own walls. She could not bear to wait until the place was furnished but intended moving in as soon as the money was paid.

A fresh tang of the sea mingled with the scent of roses in the hotel courtyard. It was June, the month of roses, with all the summer to look forward to!

The French Notaire was surprisingly young, bronzed, and even more surprisingly dressed in pristine shorts and open-necked shirt, – in keeping with the back-drop of blue sea and white sails seen through the window behind him. This easy informality delighted Mrs Hanson though it was somewhat devalued by an anxious look in his eye as he came to greet her.

'Do you speak English?' she asked as they sat facing each other across his desk. He lifted both hands apologetically. 'Ah Madame, je regrette...' So the transaction would have to be conducted in her own limited French. But no matter, all that was left now was to pay the balance of the purchase price.

As she opened her bag the Notary's look of worry deepened, – he hoped that she had been able to bring evidence of her 'Etat Civil'.

'Bien sur,' she replied, rather amused, and handed him her passport, birth certificate and marriage lines, all of which he examined carefully. 'But your Contract of Marriage, Madame? You have no Contract of Marriage?'

Mrs Hanson smiled and explained that she had not, – it was not usual in England.

The Maitre began to look desperate. 'And your husband is unable to arrive for the definitive signature?'

'At this moment my husband is in the South Indian Ocean. He is Captain of a ship.'

'Alors, il est au large!'

At large, yes! Mrs Hanson smiled again at the English implication. But the maitre was frowning so she gave him all her attention, and then could hardly believe what he was saying. The affair, he was telling her, could not be completed without her husband's presence and signature. In the circumstances it would be impossible to proceed with the purchase.

Mrs Hanson explained patiently that while her husband was at sea she was forced to deal with their financial affairs and that, as the Maitre knew, the money was already deposited in a bank of his own approval.

'Agreed, Madame, but you have no Marriage Contract, no Séparation de biens'...'

'This I do not understand!' The Maitre's attempt to elucidate reached Mrs Hanson's mind in a jumble of repetition. She was not allowed to sign for her husband because she had no 'Séparation de biens' whatever that meant. One awful possibility began to occur to her. 'You mean that I cannot take possession?'

'Madame, I regret...in your husband's absence, no.' The maitre was stating what to him was obvious, but doubted that his French was understood.

Mrs Hanson understood the last words only too well. What could she do, – with her husband separated by so many miles of ocean? She wondered aloud if the British Consul could help.

The Notaire was obviously relieved by this suggestion. He would connect Madame by telephone and the Consul could explain to her in English. Luckily Her Britannic Majesty's Pro-Consul was available and Mrs Hanson was soon listening to an English voice. 'I'm afraid I cannot deal with trouble over property,' it said.

'Ah, there is no problem there, and the balance of the purchase price is deposited in a bank here, so I quite expected to take possession, but I am told that my husband's signature is vital. He is in a ship at sea which will not even touch port for another month. Could you possibly convince the Notary that when my husband is at sea I simply have to deal with our affairs?'

'Well I can try,' said the Pro-Consul in a tone which was far from hopeful. After a lengthy exchange in French he said, 'I am sorry, it seems that the problem is your civil state under French law. You have no Marriage Contract giving you the right to sign on your husband's behalf, or a clear 'Séparation de biens' as they call it...'

'Well never mind, if I can't sign for my husband tell the Maitre that the place can be registered in my name.'

But this simple solution when put to the Notary was even more vehemently rejected. Not only was it illegal but the Maitre himself was obviously horrified that a woman who was not even allowed to sign for her husband, who had no 'Séparation de biens' should think of buying property in her own right.

'I simply can't believe my ears! said Mrs Hanson.

'I'm afraid that is how the law stands in France,' said the Consul.

'What then does he suggest we do?'

The telephone was shuttled to and fro once more. The Maitre explained that there was only one solution. If the Captain could not be present for the transfer of property he must send a sworn affidavit to nominate his wife or other representative to act for him.

'Well, I suppose I shall have to settle for that,' said the wife, 'Luckily his ship is bound for Milford Haven.'

'But Mrs Hanson, the Notary points out that he cannot act on an English document, – it will then have to be translated into French...'

'Really, you'd think I was trying to buy up a National monument! But I can easily get a translation...'

'Ah, but it must be a legal French translation, – the document will have to go to a central office in Paris to be officially translated.'

'Lord give me patience!' exclaimed the Captain's wife, seeing the precious summer slipping away into autumn. Then desperation gave her an idea. 'Perhaps to save time it could be done the other way round? Would you please ask the Maitre if he can make out an acceptable affidavit in French which can be sworn before a Notary Public in England?'

The receiver was shuttled once more and the Notaire's face brightened. It was easy to understand that he was agreeing to prepare a 'Pardevant' for Madame to take to her husband. 'Yes,' the Consul confirmed, 'The Maitre will have the Pardevant ready tomorrow if that is convenient.'

'As convenient as anything in the circumstances, I suppose. I am very grateful...'

'Sorry I couldn't do more to help...the French are like that, I'm afraid...'

'Well you should know!'

There was a deprecating diplomatic chuckle in reply, and there the Consular intervention ended.

However the Notaire was looking worried again, puzzled, hesitant and then impelled to express another doubt. How, he asked, would it be possible for an English Notary to deal with a French legal document?

'Monsieur Maitre, please don't unquiet yourself,' said Mrs Hanson, French idiom leaping to mind in exasperation. 'English lawyers have been using French since the days of William of Normandy!' This was an inspired rather than an educated guess, but very satisfying to make.

Captain Hanson brought his ship safely to Milford Haven and entered the port on the high tide at 0500. The huge vessel was manoeuvred to a jetty, hoses connected and gangway lowered. Oil was soon belching into the terminal for a turn-round of no more than forty-eight hours. When Mrs Hanson climbed aboard in the wake of a surge of port agents, surveyors, Customs officers and ship-chandlers, her husband was already sitting at the head of a long table dealing with these visitors. The wife sat quietly at one side waiting and by eleven o'clock the Captain was free to kiss his spouse and be led ashore.

The solicitor's office was the converted ground floor of a late-Victorian dwelling house, with freshly whitened steps to the front door, black railings, well-polished brass plate and doorknocker. The Notary was as informally dressed as the Notaire but in baggy grey flannels and comfortably patched tweed jacket. The couple sat facing him across a wide desk as he glanced through the Pardevant's three pages of legal French while the situation was explained. Then, without further comment he asked them to wait a moment and disappeared into an inner office.

The Captain was comfortable, content with a brief respite from ship's cares, quietly enjoying this novel experience. Having to swear an affidavit to permit his wife to spend money! Splendid country, France! He would be happy to spend his leaves there, – roll on September!

But Mrs Hanson waited uneasily. Would the attorney accept or reject the Pardevant? Why had she made such a wild uneducated guess without checking, – especially about Wales. The Norman Conquest was long ago and far away, – and yet...

The solicitor returned after ten long minutes. 'Now we can proceed, he said, 'You must both sign at the foot of each page, your wife first, Captain.'

The wife signed, one page, two, and on the third page she saw that the solicitor had typed in his legal blessing, in French:

"Fait et passé a Milford Haven, Dyfed, Grande Bretagne. Geoffry Hill, notaire par autorité Royale, dument admis et assermenté."

Mrs Hanson signed her name with a triumphant flourish underneath.

The document was passed to her husband. 'Have you read the declaration?' asked the Welsh Maitre.

'Yes, I've read it,' replied the Captain, signing away cheerfully, 'Couldn't understand a word of it of course...Hrmm!!' It was obvious that his ankle had been kicked by an infuriated wife.

But the Welsh Maitre seemed unconcerned, turning a deaf legal ear to this little domestic contretemps, barely concealing his amusement while he pressed the official stamp on each page and endorsed them with his signature.

(This was the author's own experience, written up as an example of the different law and the different attitude to law in France and England. The surname was changed for possible publication in The European)

A MARRIAGE OF CONVENIENCE

This is a true story, told me by my husband's half-sister, Eva, who came from Poland to visit us in south-western France in 1984, escaping briefly on holiday out of the Cold-War, – which at that time seemed likely to last for ever. And her tale could hardly have been told against a more contrasting backdrop, the sunshine and sea of our rich summer life in Arcachon.

Eva's story was of her friend, Krystyna who, when Poland was sealed off during the savage suppression of the Solidarity trade-union in 1981, had risked a marriage of convenience with an Austrian so that she might travel freely out of the country. Not, it need hardly be said, to visit she man she was marrying to obtain the passport, – but to join her lover who had already escaped into Austria.

By 1984 when travel restrictions were eased a little we obtained a French visa for Eva with which she could apply for a Polish 'passport' so called, permitting her to leave her own country for just one trip. But even then the currency restriction was still total and neither dollars nor foreign currency nor the worthless Polish zloty could be taken out of the country. And the tedious process of obtaining this one trip passport had taken Eva so long that we could hardly believe the telegram which eventually named the day of her arrival.

Incorrectly as it happened, – she fell into our doorway a day earlier than expected, penniless and exhausted, having carried a hefty suitcase two kilometres from the station.

Her train journey which involved changing across Paris had been eighteen hours long from East Berlin where she had broken the journey to stay with a friend, – and a nightmare experience that had been, she gasped, as she collapsed on our doorstep. 'Such trouble there was to get out of East Germany again!' she exclaimed, 'We think Poland is a Police state, but East Germany! Never will I risk another visit!'

Eva was too tired to eat, let alone relate adventures so she was put to bed with a hot drink and slept fifteen hours through which made me somewhat uneasy. But she did emerge next day, a new person, wearing brief shorts topped by a stunning shirt of simple pale blue cotton, which had the unmistakable stamp of haute couture.

'Eva, you look prettier than ever!' I said as we kissed, 'And what a fabulous blouse!'

'Yes, I am so pleased with it. I bought it in East Berlin with my smuggled zloty, very cheap, not more than half a pound in English money I think…'

'Never!' I exclaimed, deciding at once that if the German Democratic Republic was producing garments of grande classe for fifty pence a piece then there I must risk going, police state or not, to replenish my wardrobe. 'Their shops must be gorgeous, Eva!'

'No, the shops are very poor. I bought this in a street market. The people get presents, you see, from relatives in West Germany, and sell what they do not need, – the most beautiful clothes.'

'Ah, so that explains it, – a jumble sale in East Berlin! But you say you had trouble getting away? What happened?'

'It makes me shiver to think, – and so angry I cannot tell…'

'You'd better have your breakfast first then.' So Eva ate her breakfast while I was preparing the evening meal, – our time-scale having got rather out of step, – and food and drink soon put her into fighting trim, ready to enlarge on her own experience. But her friend Krystyna's adventure of marrying a man she had never even met in order to travel freely was not yet so much as hinted.

Having obtained her one-trip passport Eva was determined to make the most of it and as the train journey could be broken at no extra cost she decided to stay for a few days on the way out with a friend who had married a German living in East Berlin. Her East German visa was valid for a whole month so she also hoped to spend another a day or two there on her return journey.

In Warsaw Eva climbed aboard the Paris section of the famous East-West express which had already travelled through the night from Moscow. She had no trouble leaving the train in East Berlin where she spent a pleasant few days with her friends and on the evening of her departure they drove her to the station in good time. This was then around ten o'clock, after dark, and her friends did not accompany her on to the platform, – judging by what followed they may well have feared to do so.

Eva was puzzled to see the train's time of arrival on the information board, but no time of departure. However at that moment the train arrived. Passengers alighted and Eva located the Paris coach, but when she attempted to climb aboard she found herself looking up the barrel of a gun, aimed at her by an angry soldier guarding the door from the inside. Eva tried to explain to him that she had merely broken her journey from Warsaw to Paris, but this only made the man more belligerent and abusive, prodding her with his gun and screaming at her to go back to Poland.

Eva was very frightened, in despair at the prospect of having to return to Warsaw with her once-only passport. She searched around for help, but there seemed to be only soldiers to appeal to, and not knowing what else to do she left the station in tears. To her great relief she found that her friends were still in the car-park, – they had been waiting to see the train depart.

Although very nervous about entering the station, they were brave enough to make further enquiry and were told that Eva had been mistaken in thinking that she could re-join the train at this East Berlin station where she left it. She should have gone to the next station, the Freidrichstrasse, a station specially constructed to screen passengers leaving the country, – built and defended like a fortress to prevent unauthorised people boarding the train.

The Freidrichstrasse was the last station on the line inside the Berlin Wall, about two kilometres away, and after losing so much time over the enquiry Eva was driven there at breakneck speed.

But there had been no need for hurry, – this East-West so-called express takes an inordinate time to traverse all the eastern frontier stations. One hour had been lost at the Russo-Polish border, another on entering East-Germany at Frankfurt-on-Oder, and in those days for the critical transit of the Berlin Wall the passengers were carefully re-checked in case they had multiplied or changed identity on the way.

The whole train was searched inside and out, under the seats, along the roof, – in the luggage van to make sure nobody was sewn into a mail-bag, and under the train itself in case an escapee might be discovered clinging to a bogey.

So Eva arrived in plenty of time. Her friends wished her farewell once again and watched her being sucked into the maw of armed guards with no way of knowing her fate. They lived in the terror of a closed regime, in fear of sudden disappearance, and after a week or so of waiting for news of Eva's safety their anxiety was brought home to us in our peaceful French home by a frantic telegram routed via Warsaw for secrecy. Eva had casually sent them a postcard which took many weeks to get back to East Berlin.

Inside the station Eva's papers were checked, her through ticket was minutely examined and accepted. Then she was escorted by armed guards along a platform on which soldiers were standing every few yards with machine guns at the ready, and she was finally allowed into the Paris section of the train.

By then Eva had lost all desire to stop off in East Berlin on her return journey but nevertheless was seething with indignation at having discovered that her month's East German visa had been automatically cancelled on exit.

Beyond the 'Wall' there was a mere ten-minute stop in West Berlin and the rest of the journey was uneventful. There were no more checks at the borders, Eva said, officials simply walked along the train as it ran, glancing into her compartment and not even asking to see her papers.

'Tell me, Eva, how is your friend Krystyna?' I asked while we were clearing the evening meal. I had only met her once but the girl had a memorable quality.

'Oh, I have so much to tell! Such a story of Krysia's wedding!'

'Krystyna married!' I exclaimed, very amused, remembering the girl's antipathy to marriage, about which Eva had told me much. I also recalled that her mother, Pani Halina, had gone to work in Vienna after the father died, leaving Krystina in possession of their flat in Warsaw in which Krysia's boy-friend, Vlodek, had been installed soon after Pani Halina's departure.

Eva then had sounded rather envious of Krystyna's flat, or possibly her independence, – but I loved the little house in which Eva lived with her mother, – it is so unusual to come across an individual house in Warsaw.

This colony of small dwellings had been built after the war to house Russian so-called 'Advisors', had been thrown together by forced labour at a time when it seemed impossible that anything could be built at all in the chaos of the ruined city. Brick had been slapped roughly on brick and the mortar which oozed out between them like the filling in a layer-cake had been left to congeal with no attempt at pointing or stucco.

Subsequently the houses were occupied by Poles and when we visited Warsaw in 1965 Eva's mother and father had been allocated two rooms in this house. They shared the kitchen and a primitive bathroom with a bevy of other people who, as I remember well, sat with their own door open so that for necessary journeys within we were forced to run the gauntlet past tiers of curious eyes. The kitchen had been kept clear for the occasion by a negotiated truce in the hostilities which inevitably raged over common ground.

On our next visit some years later central Warsaw had changed beyond recognition with a sky-scraper hotel and a shopping-precinct pleasantly laid out and quite well-stocked with goods. Charming plantations of trees refreshed the eye in every open space, though the drive from the centre through streets of gaunt flats was dreary enough until we came upon this oasis, this colony of small dwellings almost buried in the profusion of foliage which typifies Polish gardening.

My father-in-law had died in the meanwhile and now not only did Eva and her mother have complete possession of the house but Eva was actually negotiating to buy it. 'Council' houses and flats being on sale in Communist Poland long before such a revisionist idea was thought of in England.

The house itself was grown about with trees. We entered by a wicket gate in a perimeter fence thick with leaves, along a narrow path between a confusion of fruit-bushes, Buddlea and sunflowers to the main door on the side of the house overhung by a great apple-tree. The path led on past the door where a glimpse of rough grass surrounded by trees gave an impression of limitless distance. Looking up at the house I saw that the congealed mortar still oozing out between the bricks in suspended motion had survived nearly thirty years of weather and mellowed, giving the house a curious charm.

Then we entered the house, seeing for the first time its limited extent. Opposite on the ground floor was Pani Zofia's room looking on to the garden. A passage led past the bathroom and kitchen to a larger living room at the front of the house in which was a great black heating stove. Then Eva took us up a tiny staircase to show us the small room in which we were to sleep, and in passing she opened another door into the roof which sloped down at the back of the house. It was a capacious storeroom, very perilous from having no floor with a few planks laid along the beams to shelves sparsely filled with Pani Zofia's preserves.

Then Eva showed us her own sanctum, a larger room with a dormer window, ceiled but still with a cosy feeling of being within the roof. Recessed shelves tapered into the apex and held a richer collection of books than I could have afforded, – Eva told us that they were very cheap in Poland.

A divan bed nestled in the opposite alcove and there beside it was Eva's greatest achievement yet, only just installed. A telephone! For which she had fought persistently and waited long.

Altogether the house appeared enchanting and we went to bed that night feeling that prosperity was at last reaching Poland, which indeed it was at the time, – in the form of massive bank-loans. But in those days we had heard little about the hazards of high finance, the ineptitude of governments, the cupidity of officials, or the idiotic optimism of bankers which fuelled it all.

Eva had lent me an illustrated book to read in bed, 'The Land of Copernicus' in English. But the ideological fervour of the text soon produced drowsiness and I drifted off to sleep soothed by the murmur which reached us through the thin partition wall of Eva revelling in her new facility, having an interminable telephone conversation.

The subdued sound had a soporific effect on me. Not so however on my husband who tossed and fretted that anyone could be running up such a telephone bill even though he wasn't paying for it. I only restrained him with difficulty from banging on the wall, but I was happy to see that when he started holding forth in the morning his half-sister refused to be browbeaten. She replied crisply that after going to so much trouble to get the telephone installed she had no intention of economising on local calls which were very cheap in Warsaw.

After Eva finished work in the afternoon we met her at a famous café above a shop in the main street, Marzal Kowska. It had large windows looking out into trees and a luxurious décor within, gold paint and chandeliers, as I remember. This was one of the examples of free enterprise allowed at that time if limited to six employees.

We were eager to sample their famous ice-cream sundae served in huge goblets which, we were told by Eva's friends who joined us, was called Ambrosia and was never twice the same. It was a mixture of whatever fresh fruit was in season, they said, and this was the very best time of year.

Our goblets of Ambrosia arrived, and the first taste made me agree that no other word could do justice to it. The ice-cream itself was delicious and on that day was garnished with a melange of wild strawberries and bilberries swirled together with sweetened sour cream and laced with liqueur. An unforgetable taste.

And among Eva's friends was Krystyna, an oustandingly attractive girl whose appealing expression gave her face a charm which lingered afterwards in my mind, linked with the delicate wild taste of the bilberries and wood-strawberries so that I was always interested to hear more of her.

Thus I heard about Krystyna's mother having gone to live in Vienna, and Krysia's enviable flat, and Vlodek's installation in it, and Krystyna's devotion to him. 'They will soon be married?' I had supposed then, – my mind still running along quaint old-fashioned lines.

'Never!' exclaimed Eva.

'You mean Vlodek doesn't want to marry her?'

'Oh Vlodek would like very much, but Krysia will never agree. Marriage spoils men. She is determined never to marry! And I too!' added Eva in the severe tone she had used to her brother when he scolded her about using the telephone.

Even so, remembering these determined words, my exclamation in Arcachon some years later was more amused than surprised. 'So her boy-friend persuaded her at last! What was his name? I forget.'

'Vlodek, – and persuade her he did, – to marry an Austrian, a stranger she had never met...'

'Good heavens Eva! I can hardly believe it! Why? What happened?'

'It is such a strange story, – no wonder you don't believe...but I must tell it properly from the beginning...'

'Let's finish the dishes then, and you can tell me over coffee!'

Our man of the house, a retired sea captain, my husband, Eva's much older brother, – strictly speaking her half-brother, if a man of his bulk could be so described – and if indeed it were in his character to be anything by halves, – this man was just then immersed in a tangle of wires looking for a fault in his musical equipment, a task which usually kept him amused for hours. But Eva and I were hardly settled when the music began and we were only too happy to flop out and listen. So that evening was lost to Krystyna, but on the next day the story did begin.

On the following morning our Captain cast his professional eye over the weather which was just about perfect and decided that this was a day for sailing on our nearest lake at Sanguinet. So after breakfast Eva and I threw some lunch into the cold-box while he was hitching the boat-trailer to the car, and off we set.

A few kilometres south of Arcachon the vast sweet-water lakes of Sanguinet and Biscarosse lie inland from the sea, separated and protected from the Atlantic Ocean by a ridge of wooded hills. The largest of the lakes is Sanguinet, quite an inland sea boasting four small ports. We drove to the nearest, driving down a little road where the view opened up between trees of the Beau Rivage Hotel by the side of a little hard.

But there wasn't a breath of wind. The water was flat calm, reaching out pale blue into deeper blue, paling again into limitless horizon, and the boats at anchor near the shore were floating on reflections which hardly trembled.

As the car pulled up by the hard Eva leapt out. There was a delicate light scent in the air. 'The lime trees are in flower!' she exclaimed.

We let the captain drive on round the curve of the bay to his favourite launching spot and we found that the lime trees which hang over the stream that empties into the little harbour were heavy with scent and alive with bees.

We stood on the arched wooden bridge over the stream looking at the black sinister water beneath us. 'I wouldn't like to swim here,' said Eva wrinkling her nose.

'Come,' I replied, and led her back over the slipway to the lake edge proper where golden sand showed through water which was crystal clear. We waded around the edge of the beach causing little ripples in the water which was warm besides being soft and fresh, and when the sound of a bell striking noon came over the water Eva paused to look back. The view had widened behind us showing a church spire rising out of a billowing sea of trees, the line of boats moored to the jetty and a few more at anchor on the calm water.

The tranquillity of the scene was heightened by some activity on the terrace of the Beau Rivage Hotel. Tables had been laid for lunch and a few guests were already consulting the menu for their most serious meal of the day, making our cold-box seem cold comfort and giving me a pang of envy. 'It is delightful here,' said Eva.

'Yes, it is charming, though it hardly compares with Ruciana Nida,' I replied, recalling a summer on the Mazurian lakes.

'With Mazuria nothing can compare,' said Eva complacently, 'But this is beautiful too.

We were roused by a sharp nautical bark to 'Look alive there and help me to launch the dinghy!' We leapt to the command and waded into the water until the little boat was floating. The mast was stepped, the sails hoisted and sheets adjusted. 'But there is no wind,' said Eva.

'Hold fast, landlubber while I climb aboard,' said our sailor, 'and you will see!' And sure enough the sails filled with an imperceptible breeze and the Captain ghosted out on the lightest of light airs into the middle of the lake. But there his sails began to wilt.

'Now Eva, is our chance,' said I, 'You can tell me all about Krystyna.' We waded ashore and settled ourselves on a grassy bank above a crescent of sand. Eva adjusted a leaf under her sunglasses to protect her nose and this is the tale she told.

It seemed that Krystyna's Vlodek was driving about in a near wreck of a car and at that time was considered lucky to have even a wreck to drive around in. But to buy a better car he needed dollars, – the only workable currency in Communist Poland, needless to say, was the capitalist U.S. dollar.

When I last heard of him Eva had described Vlodek as being blessed by fortune, having a beautiful flat to live in, a devoted girl to love him, and no mother-in-law. Not to mention being cared for overall from cradle to grave by a socialist regime in which unemployment was not recognised.

It was true that the socialist economy was not then quite perfected, but there was visible improvement, goods were beginning to appear in the shops, Poland was making Fiat cars under licence a few of which came onto the home market, allocated by lot to employees. Soon after our visit Eva had been lucky enough to draw by lot the smallest Polski Fiat at the cheap official price and could have sold it again for many times as much in dollars. But she could not bear to lose it in spite of a door parting from its hinges on the first day.

Nobody then realised that the country was enjoying a hopeful spending spree on borrowed money, – until the interest began to mount up, when it was found that the wheels of industry had not been turning as profitably as planned. Many in fact had not even begun to turn before the money ran out. There is nothing paltry about Communist planning, – factories had been conceived on the same heroic scale as their sculpture and the Polish countryside became littered with unfinished factories, – vast skeletal monuments to this heroic vision, – abandoned when the capital dried up.

Conditions went from bad to worse, more money had to be borrowed, some got into the wrong hands or was otherwise frittered by over-manning, poor management and top-heavy bureaucracy. Very little reached the pockets of the workers and that little bought less and less. Endlessly urged to work harder they worked as little as they could get away with, – joking as usual: 'They pretend they are paying us and we pretend we are working!'

So Vlodek was ambitious to get out of Poland for a year or two to earn some foreign currency. Then occurred the heady mirage of the success of the trade-union Solidarity, when it appeared that the regime was at last relaxing its grip, until there came upon them like a thunderclap the clamp-down which Eva spoke of as 'Jarazelski's war'

'But surely you were expecting something of the sort to happen?' I asked, recalling that western commentators had foreseen the inevitable.

'We not only didn't expect it, – we hadn't the least idea what was happening when it did happen,' said Eva.

She told me that she was having a pleasant chat with her friend Alusia on the telephone late on that Saturday night (I could imagine!) when suddenly the line went dead, just on midnight as she realised afterwards. She checked that the plug had not been pulled loose and tried dialling again without result. Finally she went to sleep, puzzled by the telephone fault but not at all suspicious.

On Sunday morning at Mass she became aware of an infectious unease among the congregation. The priest did not give the expected sermon but simply said that prayers must be said for the safety of their country, without further explanation. When the Mass was over Eva ran to the Presbytery and begged the priest to tell her what had happened.

'My dear child,' he replied, 'I cannot tell you more. Indeed I do not know. Go home to your mother and try not to alarm her. Stay indoors today and go to work as usual tomorrow. Above all behave normally.'

Eva went home and switched on the radio. The usual programme was replaced by music. There was no news. Then on the hour General Jarazelski came on the air, appealing to the people to support their country in its hour of peril. No explanation. There was no news all day long, only music with the General's speech repeated at intervals. But in the evening there was one sinister change on television, – the familiar announcers were now dressed in army uniform.

The telephone remained dead and Eva said they could not guess what the peril might be. The capitalist threat in which nobody believed but which they were armed to the teeth to repel? Or their worst nightmare, a Soviet invasion as in Hungary?

The next morning Eva took a tram as usual into central Warsaw and found the streets filled with soldiers and tanks stationed at every crossroad. To her great relief the soldiers were Polish though it was evident that their guns were trained on their own people and they looked ready to use force at the slightest provocation.

Later when Eva was returning home in the tram during the rush hour she saw soldiers firing tear-gas canisters to disperse a small crowd and when people opened their windows in nearby flats to see what was going on the soldiers lobbed gas-canisters into them without hesitation.

The tram was moving with a man running after it pursued by soldiers, – the passengers shouted to the driver who slowed down and the man was hauled aboard. The doors shut as the tram accelerated and they escaped.

Eva's description could hardly have been more vivid, I knew the very street she described. But the quiet of midday France, the heat and shade, the peace of Sanguinet, itself ephemeral and diaphanous, anaesthetised my imagination. Somehow I could not relate to the horror. I murmured an inadequate stupid comment and Eva sat up.

Tiny transparent waves were beginning to ripple over the sand with the first stirrings of the breeze which usually springs up around one o'clock. 'As for Vlodek,' Eva said, adjusting the leaf on her nose, 'he decided that life in Poland was no longer possible and he determined to get away.'

'He was an activist?' I exclaimed.

'No, of course not,' Eva replied somewhat witheringly, 'If he had been an activist he would never have wished to leave his country!' There were times during her story when this young woman made me feel very naïve.

Out in the middle of the lake our sailor now had plenty of wind in his sails and although the breeze was dead off shore he was beating back towards us. Eva and I had missed our pre-lunch swim, we hurried to unload the cold-box from the car, laid the picnic table and opened the wine, but our little ship was still some distance from the shore. Eva and I drank some wine and then as we watched the dingy putting about again she exclaimed, 'Let us swim out to tow him in!

It was nice not to lose our swim after all and I found it all the more enjoyable with a glass of Bordeaux supérieur inside me. The lake is clear and shallow for a long way out over sand and is very warm. But we had to swim beyond the line where the shallow sand ends and the lake drops suddenly into back depths in which it is said there are drowned prehistoric villages, – and live prehistoric monsters I shouldn't wonder. A black depth so scary I don't usually venture beyond that line, – but good red wine spurns monsters and on I swam.

Eva, swimming strongly, reached the boat first and caught the painter and towed. I tried to pull on the painter too as they passed but I'm not sure that Eva, getting her feet into the sand at last, did not tow us all in. The dingy was beached, we tumbled ashore, dried off and sat round the table to enjoy ham and crusty bread and salad and cold fried sausages. There was fruit of course, and we finished off the wine with a delectable Brie made from double cream, which we all agreed was a memorable cheese, or would have been but that I forgot to take note of the marque and was never able to find it again.

'So what did Vlodek do?' I asked when we had settled down again. (Eva's story came along steadily once begun)

'He decided to go to Austria.'

'However did he manage to escape?'

'Oh Vlodek is not the escaping type, he went out legally. He got himself a passport.'

'But I understood all travel had been stopped!' I exclaimed, knowing the difficulty Eva had to get a passport even when it was allowed.

'As I've told you, Vlodek was resourceful. He bribed an official...' Eva lowered her hand behind her back as she spoke, with the palm cupped upwards, 'Vlodek knew someone in the Ministry which deals with jobs abroad. Anything can be done with money in Poland if you know whom to pay.' That Eva was so familiar with the pantomime of bribery and could speak with such weary cynicism revealed to me suddenly, for the first time, the extent of corruption in her country.

Poland's outstanding success in the post-war years had been the training of first-class doctors, engineers, technicians, – and musicians too, whose high standard, and cheapness, if they were paid in U.S. dollars, became much in demand over most of the world. So the Polish government, quite as eager to lay its hands on dollars as its citizens, set up two departments, technical and professional, to exploit the export of this expertise. These departments obtained work-permits from other countries, and then issued exit permits 'passports' so-called, to selected candidates for limited periods. And from these candidates they exacted thirty per cent of the dollars they earned, for the privilege of being allowed out of their own country! The passports might be renewed yearly, but as there was always a queue of applicants waiting to take their turn malpractices inevitably flourished, and nepotism and bribery added themselves to the list of qualifications required.

It was with straight bribery that Vlodek obtained his passport although he had no qualifications, technical or otherwise, and it was clear from Eva's account that there was no job waiting for him in Austria. Once there he had to fend for himself along with other escapees who were slipping over the border, dangerously, illegally, to claim political asylum, – which Vlodek had every intention of doing later, thus severing his connection with Poland for good.

Having used all his dollar savings to obtain his passport Vlodek travelled to Austria penniless, but he was going to Krystina's mother, Pani Halina who was by then established in her own flat in Vienna.

I must say the more I heard of Pani Halina the more my heart warmed towards her. She was an intellectual woman, so Eva said, who had felt an urge to see the world after Krystina's father died and decided to go to Austria to earn a living in the only occupation her work-permit would allow. 'Housekeeping' as Eva termed it, and there she discovered a freedom of life which seemed hardly credible, and which was certainly not concerned with politics.

In Poland people had been allowed to grumble freely enough provided they did not manifest publicly or publish their complaints, but Pani Halina's constraint had been the drudgery of domestic life, long hours of work outside the home, queuing and shortages, trying to make-do without the most ordinary necessities. In addition there was obviously some domestic trouble which Eva only hinted at, – and knowing her daughter's determination not to marry one could only suppose that Pani Halina's marriage had been far from easy.

Pani Halina was dazzled by the abundance and prosperity in Vienna. Shortage and hardship had given her an extra dimension of appreciation. Eva said she discovered material comforts which she had never even dreamed of, – supermarkets stuffed with food and curious often puzzling items of hardware, – and yet she watched with amazement local housewives, glutted by plenty, hurrying from shelf to shelf with strained abstracted expressions.

Whereas Pani Halina now revelled in being paid handsomely for the same 'housekeeping' which had been taken for granted in married life. With the freedom of 'owning' her own money she could do what she chose with her earnings. She was actually able to save as well as to live comfortably, and to buy dollars to send to Krystyna when she could find anyone able to carry them into Poland. There the Communist regime had even set up 'dollar shops' filled with scarce items in order to lay its own needy hands on some of the foreign currency which flowed into Poland from generous relatives abroad.

Krystyna's dollars, as it happened, went straight into Vlodek's car-fund, and it was with these, mainly, that he was able to bribe his way out of Poland during the clamp-down of Jarazelski's 'war.

I remembered how worried we were about not hearing from Eva during that time when Poland had been so suddenly and dramatically isolated from the rest of the world, with all communications cut. Even the post was stopped and later on delayed by censorship for months at a time. So I could imagine Pani Halina's relief when Vlodek, the escapee, arrived out of the void to take refuge with her, bringing news that Krystyna was alive and well. And from my own experience of Polish hospitality I could easily imagine the welcome he received.

But I was intensely curious to know how Vlodek coped. How does anyone begin to make money in a foreign country when it is so difficult to make a living in one's own where no work-permit is required? Eva did not know she could only answer my questions by repeating that Vlodek could turn his hand to many jobs, and of course he had Pani Halina's support, not to mention her flat to live in.

So there was Vlodek, making money as he could, determined not to return to Poland, living with his girl-friend's mother. But time was slipping by and they were both concerned to find a safe way for Krystyna to join them, a logistical problem which was more difficult for Vlodek to solve outside the country. But he did not doubt that once the route was arranged Krystyna would be happy to share his self-imposed exile.

However their tenuous communication showed that she was becoming reluctant to leave Poland with no hope of return. Her mother had gone away legally and could return if she wished. So indeed could Vlodek, but if he once claimed political asylum there was no hope of being allowed back. It was not the uncertainty of the outside world that gave Krystyna pause but the certainty of permanent exile. The Iron curtain was more firmly shut than before and everyone expected that the Cold War would go on for ever. This dilemma of never being allowed back hardened Krystyna's resolution and she refused to think of leaving Poland unless she could do so legally. It was perhaps her stubborn attitude which made Vlodek all the more determined.

In Austria there had been much publicity about the traffic in marriages of convenience. At that time only a male Austrian could confer the privilege of residence to a spouse but when a feminist law was about to be passed giving women equality with men it became clear to the government that this particular right must be abolished for both sexes equally. To prevent young males from the Eastern block flooding into the country in even greater numbers.

The publicity gave Vlodek the idea of arranging such a marriage for Krystyna before the law was changed, and he made her a tentative 'proposal' – provided he could find an acceptable candidate who would undertake the romantic task for a reasonable fee.

Krystyna told Eva of this 'proposal' and both girls nearly collapsed with laughing. How could Vlodek raise the money? How could he approve of the man? A character prepared to sell his name for a relatively small sum would hardly be a suitable candidate for the love of one's life! Moreover the new Austrian law was due to take effect from September 1st of that year, 1983, and as it was already mid-July Vlodek's proposal appeared to be stillborn. Krystyna gave it no more thought.

Then suddenly, at the end of the month she received catalytic news. Vlodek had found a bridegroom! A man who was prepared to travel to Poland to marry her, – and if Krystyna was willing Pani Halina had agreed to put up the money! But the decision must be made at once to arrange the ceremony before the Austrian deadline.

Our heroine had no time for prudent or second thoughts. She had to make up her mind to tie herself legally to a man she didn't know, a man bribed by a relatively paltry sum, (Eva had no idea how much the marriage fee was) – and this wedding she must organise and face alone. There was indeed comfort that it was Vlodek who had chosen the bridegroom, and that her mother, in offering to pay her dower, was obviously prepared to trust the man.

Her mother's blessing weighed much with Krystyna but she felt very reluctant to accept her hard-earned savings. Yet to refuse them would be to slam the door on adventure and lose an extraordinary chance.

And so Krystyna agreed.

Krystyna alerted Eva and their mutual friend Alusia, inviting them to be witnesses at her wedding. The news electrified the girls. Local telephone calls had been restored so the wires hummed between them into the night and much burnt-wheat coffee was drunk in cafes as they discussed what needed to be done in so short a time. Booking the ceremony was of critical importance and when Krystyna succeeded in booking a slot just in time, – three o'clock on the last Saturday in August they rejoiced.I am not sure that Vlodek would have been altogether gratified by the enthusiasm caused by the marriage which he had arranged.

But it was delightful to see Eva's eyes light up as she told this part of her story, – making me suspect that none of these maidens were feminist through to the core, and that however much they disapproved of the married state they had no objection to a wedding. By abolishing husbands they had been sadly deprived of the ceremony.

It was exclusively an affair of the three girls, and Krystyna now felt the advantage of not having relations to bother about, – no fear of outraged uninvited aunts. And after the success of fixing the day came the engrossing problem of what to wear.

Although Eva described all their dresses in detail no clear picture remains in my mind except that Krystyna was to wear blue and the two witnesses planned their finery to complement the bride's outfit. 'Just like bridesmaids,' I suggested.

'No, not at all like,' Eva exclaimed, 'I have seen so often, – being forced to wear a dress of the bride's choice, never mind if it suits you or not, and some silly posy on the head. No thank you! We discussed. Krysia made herself a pale blue dress with material her mother had sent long ago, – you should have seen, – she is so clever at making, – I am not.'

And Krystina wore a charming hat with a floppy brim, and was determined to carry a spray of flowers, – which were very difficult to find, so Eva told me, trying to describe them. Later when she noticed some giant gladioli in a flower shop she exclaimed, 'There they are! Krystina's wedding flowers!' She saw my disbelief. 'It is true,' she said, 'only hers were not longer than my fingers!' And sure enough when I checked in my gardening book there they were listed. Fortunately these miniature gladioli were tracked down in time, and with such engrossing details Krystyna approached her marriage vows.

Then of course there was the food. After the ceremony the bridegroom would have to be fed so a wedding feast with Eva and Alusia was planned, – if only to pass the time safely. The bridegroom was to stay the night in Krystyna's spare bedroom, and the two witnesses planned to camp out in the living-room to guard against any threat of 'consummation.'

There was quite as much excitement in garnering the provisions as in the planning of raiment, – only those who have known desperate shortage can appreciate the delight, the sense of occasion that such a feast can give. Who can arouse the same enthusiasm for turkey now it can be bought in supermarkets all the year around?

Eva produced the cake, her one speciality in the food line, – which was no more a wedding-cake than she a bridesmaid, but all the more delectable for that. She had made one for us in earlier years, big as a cartwheel, eighteen inches across, made of something between biscuit and sponge, sandwiched together and masked with soft creamy chocolate perfumed with liqueur. This cake melts in the mouth, which can hardly be said of a slice of wedding-cake.

For such ingredients and other exotic items precious dollars were expended at the government dollar store which had been set up to cream some profit from those desirable greenbacks which flashed between the hands of the citizens. But in late August wild mushrooms could be gathered and a delicious dish made of them.

Eva's car also had to be made ready, not with ribbons but simply by finding enough petrol, much more difficult, – and being made more roadworthy, which was totally impossible. Her little Polish Fiat was in sad need of a new battery, nowhere to be found. The best Eva could mange was to have the old one recharged and scrounge a few litres of petrol.

But over these pleasing preparations lurked the sinister shadow of the unknown bridegroom, looming more formidable as the great day approached. Krystyna sometimes found it impossible to believe that he would really materialise. She was often uneasy at the thought of the ordeal, the stranger standing beside her at the ceremony, sitting at her wedding-feast, sleeping in her home, though not, thank God, in her bed, – before he could be safely despatched back to Austria on the Sunday.

What would he look like, they all wondered, – this unknown Mr X in the equation? The witnesses joked when the bride tried on her dress to show them, displaying her charming floppy hat. They conjured up the ideal bridegroom standing beside her. He must be young of course, – but not too young, – about as young as Vlodek, taller perhaps, – Vlodek was rather sturdy. And fair, to set off the pale blue dress, – fairer than Vlodek who was rather swarthy. Poor Vlodek, it was just as well that he could not hear them.

From the meagre information given to Krystyna the bridegroom had sounded dull at best. Respectable, they had told her. But impecunious obviously. So was he simply needy? Or greedy? And probably seedy too! Was he perhaps a plausible con-man who would fail to turn up? Vlodek had agreed to pay this needy or greedy man half the fee before he left Vienna, and the remainder when he returned. Supposing he simply disappeared with half the payment? There were moments when Krysia felt such reluctance and distaste for the whole sordid affair that she heartily wished he would disappear.

But Mr X did turn up, – one night sooner than expected.

On that Friday evening Eva was at home, her mind filled with speculation about the wedding on the following day, looking forward to a leisurely evening, using some specially saved soap for her bath, some precious shampoo for her hair. And just as she was turning the tap for her bath the telephone rang.

It was Krystina. 'Eva! Come quickly, – he is here! He phoned when I finished work... I have just driven to meet him...but Eva, it is hopeless! For God's sake come and help out with your German. I cannot even talk to him!'

Krystyna begged her to come as soon as possible and in no time Eva was in her car turning the ignition key from which dangled a medal of St Christopher. The starter whirred, its few remaining teeth engaged the engine which obligingly sprang to life, and Eva was away, – the impatience which is a normal feature of her driving supercharged with a fever of curiosity to meet the bridegroom, however hopeless as Krysia seemed to indicate. Poor St Christopher was in for a rough ride, – he has a hectic time of it in the Catholic cities of the world! But once again he performed his miracle of bringing Eva safely to a parking space near the bar where the happy couple awaited her.

Krystyna ran to greet Eva as she entered the door, and her eyes were shining. 'He is nice, don't you think?' she whispered as they exchanged kisses.

A tall young man was standing at the table waiting for them. A good-looking young man with a pleasant shy expression. 'But we cannot talk to each other,' said Krystyna. And as they walked towards him Eva felt that even if she had chosen him herself she could not have found a more charming complement to Krystyna's wedding outfit. He was tall, taller than Vlodek, and fair, fairer than Vlodek…' 'This is Hal, – this is Eva,' said Krystyna, struggling with her few words of German. Eva shook hands with him and they all laughed.

Hal was shy, understandably, but he was not awkward. He pulled out a chair and settled Eva into it with the innate ease of habit, – which was in itself a novel experience as Eva explained to me. It was unheard of then, she said, that a man should open a door for a woman or pull out a chair. In this and in many other respects the young Austrian seemed to have come from a forgotten world, and the girls were to revel in such little courtesies during the following weekend.

When the two were seated Hal also sat down. Eva looked at him and wondered how such a man could have been persuaded to sell his name for money. But this, she learned later, was no more than the truth.

During the previous winter Hal had been ill, Eva could not tell me what the illness was, – her account was maddeningly short of detail. But when he recovered he decided to have a look round the rest of Europe while he was convalescing. Which he did in such a leisurely manner that when he returned to Vienna in the summer he found that he had no job, a large overdraft at the bank, and a bank-manager who had run out of patience lying in wait for him.

How his need and Vlodek's became known to each other was also not clear, but Eva did know that when Vlodek first put the proposition to Hal, Hal refused. Not surprisingly, – and the more he thought about it the less he liked it. Never mind the moral aspect, he was reluctant to take on the responsibility of such a legal tie in his own country. And as for having to travel to an unknown country, risking himself in a Communist police state to tie it, he did not mind admitting to Vlodek that the mere thought made him shudder. Eva and I, discussing this, could appreciate his feelings and were agreed in our amazement that so many men were prepared to entangle themselves with the legal responsibility for relatively small sums of money.

But somehow Hal was persuaded. He was given a photograph of Krystyna, – the camera had obviously caught the appealing expression which gave her face such charm and Hal could not put it out of his mind. And the time-factor was critical, for Hal too there was no time for vacillation. With his bank-manager on one side and the deadline of Austrian law on the other he had no time for prudent thought. Also he knew and respected Pani Halna, – she did not try to persuade him, but it was there underneath. A plain old-fashioned plea for help to get her daughter out of Poland legally and freely which made him feel, especially when he looked at the girl's photograph, that he could not quite turn his back on them, – or indeed miss such an adventure. If he refused the chance would be lost, – and he would have to find some other way to placate his bank-manger.

So Hal agreed.

The two girls, sitting with him at the shabby café table did not hear this story immediately. In the meanwhile they were simply entranced by his eligible appearance, and something more besides, – as Krystyna had whispered to Eva, Hal was 'nice', and Eva told me that no word could describe him better.

His charming appearance coming as such a surprise to the girls was not perhaps in itself surprising. That Vlodek should describe his candidate's physical attributes in glowing terms could hardly have been expected from human nature, while Pani Halina's concern to stress the young man's respectability had made him sound rather dismal. In the event they were all delighted with each other, and almost intoxicated with relief, – even Hal, – perhaps especially Hal.

He was relieved to find that he had managed the journey, survived the border controls, and hadn't yet been arrested for entering the country to rob the state of one of the precious citizens it was so reluctant to part with.

In Vienna once he agreed, Pani Halina's gratitude had been reassuring, and Vlodek was triumphant that his plan had been accepted. Hal had been carried along with their enthusiasm and the excitement of boarding the international train which links Vienna and Warsaw, – so romantically named the 'Chopin Express'.

But during the long wakeful hours of the overnight journey he became filled with foreboding and wished he had never set out. His fitful sleep was disturbed by noisy stops and tedious checks at sinister frontiers, each closing grimly behind him, shutting him into regimes in which people were trapped, fearful of authority, – in which he could no longer feel confident of protection under the law.

He dozed into nightmare over the endless plains of southern Poland, shook himself awake and wished he had company. No wonder bridegrooms needed a best man to support them! He had the sardonic notion that Vlodek was escorting him in spirit as 'best man' by proxy, to stand over him to see this crazy wedding through. But the notion did not amuse him, – by that time he was heartily sick of Vlodek and wished he had never met him.

The small hours passed and early in the morning the train reached Warsaw-Gdansk station which was then the terminus of the Vienna express. Hal had to find his way about and somehow pass the whole day until it was time to telephone his bride-to-be, – that domineering fellow, Vlodek, had insisted that he came one day early. But once off the train everything seemed normal, pitifully shabby but not as drab as he expected. People were going to work, there were no soldiers in the street, – he could not even see a policeman.

And now at last he was sitting with two girls who seemed genuinely pleased to see him. Almost unbelievably, – because any fear of falling foul of authority had been equalled by fear of the embarrassment of meeting the woman to whom he was to lend his name for the most sordid of reasons. In truth he was ashamed of himself, deeply ashamed of needing the money, and deeply ashamed of the method of earning it. He had expected that however polite or grateful the bride might be she would scorn him from the bottom of her heart.

But here he was, welcomed with smiles from the most enchanting creature imaginable. Indeed both girls were charming, and far from looking on him with scorn were bubbling over with fun and good humour.

They did not sit late into the evening, the two women had to work on Saturday morning, – not that their offices would see much of either of them. Polish offices were so over-manned that it hardly disturbed the work if one person was absent from time to time, everyone took a turn to slip out to search for food or join a queue. But an appearance had to be made at eight o'clock in the morning, so the little party broke up early and Eva drove home alone. No need to camp out on Krystyna's ottoman, she was confident that Vlodek's honour and Krystyna's virtue would be safe with the young Austrian.

On the following day, the afternoon of the wedding, Eva collected Alusia and drove to Krystyna's flat. Hal and Krystyna were ready and he presented the girls with little posies of flowers, so dazzling Alusia by his easy courtesy and friendly smile that she forgot to pick up her handbag when they left the house.

The party arrived at the Town Hall in good time but there it was discovered that left behind in Alusia's handbag were the identity papers essential for a witness!

Eva had to drive her back to collect them, at breakneck speed I have no doubt. While the happy pair were left in a state of nervous anxiety, having lost both witnesses to the hazards of Warsaw traffic, the vagaries of an aged car, and the problems of re-parking, just before the ceremony. When the girls did reappear with no more than minutes to spare all four became almost hysterical with relief and could hardly restrain their laughter as they were ushered into the hall of ceremony.

The room itself was pleasing, its shining pale wood floor and furniture gave it a sunny aspect while at the same time, so Eva said, it had the almost hallowed atmosphere of a private chapel, decorated with flowers for the occasion.

The young people were even more impressed when a woman in official regalia appeared through a further doorway. She was soberly, elegantly dressed in a dark suit with heavy gold chains of office hanging from her shoulders. The woman's quiet dignity was striking but it struck Eva with fear that she must surely suspect the false nature of the marriage, must surely guess that she was being asked to preside over a mockery.

Instead she looked on the couple with admiration and obvious pleasure. They were both outstandingly attractive and appeared so radiantly happy due to the difficulty of restraining recent laughter that they really seemed, so Eva said, to be rapturously in love. Even the most cynical official might have been deceived, and Eva too felt as if under a spell while the ceremony lasted.

Krystyna's careful bridal preparations obviously added to the effect, though I am inclined to think that they would have appeared a hollow sham if the bridegroom had been the seedy suspicious character which she had expected.

In spite of themselves the four participants were impressed by the grave and simple ceremony, lacking religion though it did, and the sincerity of the woman's homily afterwards moved them very deeply.

Thus were Krystyna and Hal married.

They returned to Krystyna's flat for the wedding feast. No other guests had been invited so the party was hardly well balanced. As Eva said, it would have been unthinkable for Krysia to invite men known to Vlodek to celebrate her wedding to another man! And no one but the witnesses had been told of the affair.

However Hall might well have been dismayed by the presence of other men, and he certainly had no objection to being made much of by three women. He had produced some Austrian wine and champagne, – they were all in good appetite and the food was a great success.

The girls fell more and more under the charm of Hal's easy manner, his good-humour and innate courtesy. He did not fall on his food but noticed the needs of others round the table, and helped Krysia fetch and carry from the kitchen, not effusively but simply as if he were already at home.

Eva said that such behaviour was unheard of among Poles brought up in the Communist regime, and besides, she insisted over again, Hal was so pleasant. He laughed easily and there was much merriment as he attempted Polish words and Krystyna practised her small stock of German.

During the evening Hal suggested that he should not return to Vienna on the Sunday, and his reason for staying was surprising. Marriage did not yet allow Krystyna to travel freely out of the country although she now had the right to reside in Austria. This right enabled her, by what seemed to me an incomprehensible quirk of Polish law, to apply for a Polish so-called 'Consular passport' which would at last enable her to travel out of Poland but might well take several more months to obtain.

The first step was to get her marriage registered at the consular section of the Austrian Embassy in Warsaw on Monday morning and because of the spate of false marriages in recent years Krystyna dreaded the embarrassment of this first step. Hal had also learned something of these matters during the last days before the new law was to take effect and could see that a woman alone applying to the

Consulate without her husband's support might well encounter cynicism.

It was unthinkable that this woman who now bore his name should be exposed to humiliation and he suggested staying until Monday so that he could introduce her to the Consular officials and generally give her his protection.

Krystyna was relieved and grateful and the witnesses rejoiced! No question now of bundling the bridegroom off on the first available train, – they could plan together a whole delightful Sunday! Before they broke up it was decided that they should visit Chopin's house at Zelazowa Wola on the following day. And so Hal slept once more alone and unchaperoned in Krystyna's spare bedroom.

I have visited Chopin's house at Zelazowa Wola, a small manor house situated a few miles outside Warsaw in well-timbered country and set in four or five acres of garden. The house itself is not large and although now a museum still retains a haunting sense of occupation. The main feature is a large drawing-room on the ground-floor with wide French windows opening on to a terrace and lawn surrounded by shrubs. From this lawn the garden falls away in a series of little formal enclosures one leading into another, walled around with clipped hedges and furnished with seats and an occasional statue. All quite well-kept by Polish gardening standards which, certainly at the time we were there was not saying much. And yet to me it was that melancholy aura of neglect which gave to those little garden rooms their peculiar mystery and charm.

On summer afternoons there are concerts and when we visited the garden was far from crowded and we were able to sit on little chairs which were grouped informally on the lawn in front of the open French windows. Inside the room Chopin's music was being played on two grand pianos and my memory was the magic of watching the pianists as they played while long light mouseline curtains wafted out on the summer air with a ghostly sense of the past.

Altogether I cannot imagine a more romantic setting, – or indeed more dangerous ground, – for a young couple who had just been married and were not supposed to fall in love with each other.

Hal however, with his old-fashioned manners, displayed an old-fashioned conception of trust by scrupulously avoiding singling out his bride with any special attention which might have been taken for a marital right. His smiles and courtesies were extended to each of the girls.

With this result, – that by the Sunday evening when they returned to Warsaw to sup on the remains of the wedding feast, all three girls were in love with Hal besides one of them being positively married to him. But that one had no idea if she was specially favoured.

In those days the longest queues in Warsaw were not for food or toilet rolls but were the applicants for foreign visas who began arriving at about four o'clock every morning to wait patiently outside the Western embassies.

Hal took Krystyna to the Austrian Embassy at a civilised hour. They by-passed the pathetic queue of would-be emigrants and were let in at a special entrance where the door was only opened to admit genuine Austrian nationals.

Once inside the atmosphere was easy and friendly, – the pair were shown into a pleasant room and greeted by a consular official who invited them to sit down as if they were welcome guests and then offered coffee, – real Viennese coffee!

Eva said she did not know if there was anything special about Hal's background for what seemed to Krysia V.I.P. treatment. But on this occasion he played his marital role confidently, and his presence and Krystyna's charm were apparently convincing. Krystyna was accepted without a trace of cynicism, their marriage was duly registered and she was given her papers with the minimum of bureaucratic fuss.

On that evening Krystyna went to the station to see Hal off on the night train to Vienna, – the Chopin Express. Its very name seemed filled with romantic melancholy as they parted. The train pulled away and Krystyna was left with a desolate sense of loss, fearing that it was probably carrying Hal out of her life forever. She had given him a short letter to take to her mother, but to Vlodek she had not trusted herself to write.

On his return to Vienna Hal reported to Pani Halina and delivered Krystyna's letter. Later Vlodek met him and paid the balance of the marriage fee The money was Pani Halina's but Vlodek handled the payments and understandably perhaps, given the circumstances, behaved as if the money was his own, adopting a rather patronising air when handing over the dollars. The money was paid in dollar notes as a matter of course. No Pole would have thought of making a serious financial transaction by any other method or in any other currency.

Hal accepted the money, hating himself for doing so, and hating Vlodek even more, but he dared not refuse for Krystyna's sake. He had undertaken to marry the girl as a mere business transaction. But having found himself falling in love with her felt that he had in some way already betrayed a trust, and certainly had every intention of doing so in the future.

But he dared not implicate Krystyna by refusing the money out of hand while he was unsure of her feelings. Not that he had the slightest guilt towards Vlodek. By then he hated the sight of Vlodek and could hardly restrain his desire to thrust the dollars down the fellow's throat, together with his teeth.

If only he knew how Krystyna felt. How could she possibly bring herself to care for a man who had agreed to marry her for so shameful a reason as petty gain? The first thing he was determined to do was to find some other way to pay off his overdraft, and in the meanwhile live in hope.

Thus for a while Hal and Krystyna, legally man and wife, both continued in a romantic love-sick state, which I dare say was not without its charm. Each unsure of the other, each sometimes hopeful with the buoyancy of love and of course suffering periods of depression for the very same reason. In the meanwhile Hal was preoccupied with satisfying his bank-manager, and needless to say Krystyna was feverishly learning German.

But another factor was emerging. Eva told me that Krysia had been receiving increasingly disgruntled complaints about Vlodek from her mother. Complaints about Vlodek's selfishness and total lack of gratitude. Vlodek was still living in Pani Halina's flat and made no attempt at moving. Why indeed should he, asked Pani Halina, when he was so comfortable and well looked after? But he was taking all her care for granted. Obviously she had been happy to do everything possible to help him when he first arrived, – she had fed him, dressed him, given him money and presents including a watch, – but when he had succeeded in making money he made no offer of repayment. He not only still enjoyed free board and lodging but took all her care for granted, – as a matter of right from being one of the family. Pani Halina said she had not escaped from one domestic slavery to start all over again with the next selfish male who laid claim on her. Enough was enough!

Poor Vlodek! He did not emerge from Eva's account as a worthy or even a likeable character, but he had much against him at that time and must surely have been becoming uneasy. He was no correspondent and correspondence had not flourished between Vienna and Warsaw with the delays of censorship. Communication had been mainly through Pani Halina and difficult guarded telephone calls on occasion.

Vlodek had organised a way of getting enviable legal freedom for his love, precious dollars had been paid to a stranger and Vlodek now felt his own reward was due. But since the marriage his only reward had been increasing uneasiness, – although Eva told me that Krysia was exceedingly careful not to arouse Vlodek's suspicion of her feelings in case he might do Hal some bodily harm.

In fact none of the four participants in this little drama were especially happy during the following months while Krystyna was still as it were in political limbo, waiting for her 'Consular passport' and not yet able to visit Austria. Pani Halina was more than fed up with Vlodek. Krystyna was in a state of unrequited love, Hal equally needed requitement, if there is such a word. While in Vlodek's mind, in spite of Krystyna's caution, grew a strong suspicion that he had been cheated, and was still being cheated, – all round.

Eva was unable to satisfy my curiosity about certain aspects of the story. What did Vlodek actually do for the money he earned? How did Hal finally square his bank-manger? All she could tell me was that late in November Hal decided to visit Warsaw again, carrying the dollars with him. Were these the original dollars, I wondered? Or had those been paid into Hal's bank account to restore his credit so that he could borrow the same amount over again? This notion amused me, but Eva could not tell.

Dollars of course could be taken freely into Poland, – they had to be declared at the frontier and were welcomed. There was just the one restriction, that they could not be re-exported. But Hal was only intending to take them one way. He was returning to Warsaw to offer Krystyna his heart as well as his name, and even if she refused his love he would simply leave the dollars with her.

Krystyna had no warning of Hal's coming. He simply knocked on the door one evening, – and what happened then must be left to the imagination, – though there can be little doubt that the marriage at last was consummated! And since Krystyna could not yet travel across the border Hal had hopefully taken leave to stay for a possible honeymoon.

But they were not destined to live happily ever afterwards quite yet, or even to enjoy the bliss of their honeymoon undisturbed. Vlodek discovered that Hal had left Vienna and guessing his destination set off in furious pursuit.

I shall always remember the curious weather conditions as Eva told me the end of her story. A bank of fog was obviously rolling in from the Atlantic against the wooded heights which separate the lakes from the ocean, and every now and again a puff of this fog spilled in over the heights and sailed in a little cloud above us. Dusting us with the lightest of fine drizzle as it passed, and then in moments the sun was shining again, drying us off in seconds. More such little puffs kept drifting by and I shall never forget the almost prickly sensation of the tiny droplets dusting my sun-warmed skin. Nor am I ever likely to forget the end of Eva's story.

Once again she was unable to satisfy my curiosity about practical details. I would have given much to know how Hal had managed to get more time off after starting a new job, – or had he got his old one back? And how could Vlodek drop whatever it was he did do to earn money? And how could either young man afford the train-fares, – let alone pay their debts?

However both managed to be at leisure, to fight over a working woman who at the moment of Vlodek's arrival was languishing at her desk and eking out a modicum of work over a day which had begun at eight in the morning and would not end until three in the afternoon.

Eva told me that Vlodek burst in on Hal in the flat, though if he still had a key or burst past Hal as he opened the door, she did not know. She heard that they had a furious row but was obviously unable to give a blow-by-blow account. She seemed to think that there had been more noise than violence. Probably they both felt the need to shout abuse before indulging in fisticuffs. Vlodek was the weightier of the two but Hal had the longer reach, – both were well-matched as for hate. Hal loathed Vlodek for his scornful manner when paying over the hateful money, and of course Vlodek was in a fury with Hal for accepting it and then cheating him.

Vlodek certainly was the aggrieved party and Hal was on the defensive. But Hal's strength was in possession of the field, the girl's heart, and a legal marriage certificate. And he had done nothing dishonourable, he shouted back at Vlodek (this Eva did know) –he had acted in good faith, and then what happened had simply happened.

'Good faith!' thundered Vlodek, 'You take my money and say you have done nothing dishonourable!'

At this taunt Hal rushed to a drawer and seizing the packet of dollars thrust it into Vlodek's hands. 'I wouldn't touch your filthy dollars! They are all here, you can have them back!'

Vlodek must have been so astonished at having the money thrust upon him, and so incredulous that it still existed that he instinctively examined the packet and found that the dollars were indeed inside, the entire marriage price, – still intact. But these moments of curiosity lost him the initiative.

'Count them if you wish,' shouted Hal, 'but if you stay to do it here I will shove them down your throat!' And seizing his astonished rival he succeeded in shoving him through the door of the flat and slamming it upon him.

When Krystyna arrived home Hal was alone and triumphant, pacing about the room, still seething, fighting his fight over again, thinking how much more he could have said, wishing he had finished the job properly by throwing his rival down the stairs. Kyrstyna tried to calm him and he told her what had happened.

'Hal! You surely never gave Vlodek the dollars!'

'Of course I did! I told him I wouldn't touch his filthy money!'

'And you say Vlodek took them? And hasn't come back?'

'That's right. I threw him out!'

'But Hal, it wasn't Vlodek's money! I explained to you, – the dollars belong to my mother, – you know that as well as I do!'

Hal's triumph was shattered in a moment. Arrested in his victory march he plummeted down on the ottoman as if he had been shot. It was true, – the money did not belong to Vlodek. This fact he had known perfectly well but had forgotten in the heat of the fray.

Krystyna suddenly laughed. Her husband looked so contrite, so innocent, as he sat there cursing his folly, that she was suddenly struck by the exquisite irony of the situation. 'So Vlodek has allowed himself to be paid off!' she exclaimed.

It is very revealing, I think, that Krystyna was already convinced, even then, that her mother would never see the money again. Nor, it seemed, since I heard the story nearly a year later, had she ever done so.

'So, wasn't it funny,' said Eva to me on the beach, 'that it was Vlodek who got paid for the marriage in the end!'

Funny? It was indeed funny, in every sense of that useful little word, as any funny story I had ever heard. 'But how did Pani Halina feel about losing her money?' I asked.

'Oh she said it was well spent. In my opinion she would gladly have paid twice as much to be rid of Vlodek. And as for having Hal for a son-in-law, she was delighted. She told them that she could not have approved of him more if she had planned the marriage herself!'

And I must say that the more often I think the story over, the more I am inclined to think that that was exactly what she had done.

END